SAVAGE EMPIRE

BRI BLACKWOOD

BRETAGEY PRESS

Copyright © 2021 by Bri Blackwood

This is a work of fiction. Names, characters, places, and incidents either are the product of the author's imagination or are used fictitiously. Any resemblance to actual persons, living or dead, events, or locales is entirely coincidental. For more information, contact Bri Blackwood.

No part of this book may be reproduced in any form or by any electronic or mechanical means, including information storage and retrieval systems, without written permission from the author, except for the use of brief quotations in a book review.

The subject matter is not appropriate for minors. Please note this novel contains sexual situations, violence, sensitive and offensive language, and dark themes. It also has situations that are dubious and could be triggering.

First Digital Edition: March 2021

Cover Designed by Amanda Walker PA and Design

❦ Created with Vellum

NOTE FROM THE AUTHOR

Hello!

Thank you for taking the time to read this book. Savage Empire is a dark billionaire enemies-to-lovers romance. It is not recommended for minors and contain situations that are dubious and could be triggering. It isn't a standalone and the book ends in a cliffhanger. The next book in the series is Scarred Empire.

BLURB

He's a savage

Damien Cross treats New York City as if it's his personal playground.
    He sees.
    He touches.
    He conquers.
    He holds the fate of my family in his hands
    And makes a deal with me I can't refuse.
    He'll forgive my father's debt if he can have something in exchange: me.
    I promised myself I wouldn't get addicted, but nothing is guaranteed when you make a deal with a savage.
    Now this debt is my cross to bear.

PLAYLIST

What I've Done - Linkin Park
bad guy - Billie Eilish
I Hate Everything About You - Three Days Grace
Hate Me (with Juice WRLD) - Ellie Goulding
Monster In Me - Little Mix
Bad At Love - Halsey
ocean eyes - Billie Eilish
Paralyzer - Finger Eleven
Dance With The Devil - Breaking Benjamin
Panic Room - Au/Ra
everything i wanted - Billie Eilish
Love Is Madness (feat. Halsey) - Thirty Seconds To Mars

The playlist can be found on Spotify.

1
ANAIS

"Anais?"

I looked up from the document I was reading and smiled at the man standing at the door, but he didn't return it. I waited to see if he would walk into my office, but he stayed where he was. "Hey, Dad. What's up?"

He cleared his throat. "Are you still coming home tonight? I need to talk to you."

I almost missed his question because I was more concerned with the dark circles under his green eyes, the eyes we shared. It seemed as if he had aged overnight. A myriad of emotions crossed his face when he uttered those words, and a feeling of dread came over me that had nothing to do with his question. The expression that settled on his face was one of worry. *What is going on and what does he need to talk to me about?*

I racked my brain for a moment, trying to remember if I said I would go to my parents' home tonight. "My mind is drawing a blank. Was I?" I picked up my phone and checked the group text message I had with my family. I confirmed my father was right and sighed. The stress had to be getting to me.

"Does eight still work for you?"

I nodded, closed my eyes, and placed my index fingers on my temples. I wished the building tension away while my father remained at the door. Part of me wanted to postpone dinner and crawl into bed after work, but it was clear that Dad needed to talk to me about something important and I wanted to be there for him.

"Anais, are you okay?" I could hear him move closer to me.

"Yeah, Dad. I'm fine. Just had a long day. I'll be there tonight." I opened my eyes to find him just to the left of me. He leaned down to give me a warm hug and patted my back. My father was the CEO of Monroe Media Agency and I worked as the social media director. Our company was established over twenty-five years ago and we took care of just about everything that a company might need for their public image. I was the lead on the social media team and that included managing a few people who helped oversee the online presence of our clients.

"Don't work too hard, kiddo."

I spared him a small smile as he took a step back. "I won't. Is everything okay with you?"

He nodded his head, but it wasn't hard for me to notice his hesitation.

I debated whether to ask but refrained because I didn't know how that conversation would go. He might be more willing to talk at home. "Okay. I'll see you tonight."

Dad finally returned my smile with a small one of his own and left, closing my office door behind him. The air in the room shifted dramatically once he left. Before I could analyze the interaction further, my office phone rang.

"Monroe Media Agency, Anais speaking."

"Anais? Hi. This is Edward from CASTRA."

I held the phone away from my ear and sighed before I could stop myself. As if I didn't recognize his voice because Edward and I had talked multiple times a week about CASTRA and how to help them with their social media accounts. Even though I was the senior director of public relations and social media and managed a couple of employees who had taken on the CASTRA account, Edward still preferred to call me, no matter how many times I asked that he didn't. Since CASTRA was one of our biggest clients, I bit my tongue to stop myself from asking him once more.

"What can I help you with today?"

He rattled off a couple of issues, which could have easily been sent to me in an email and hung up the phone. I placed it back down on the hook and groaned. A quick glance at my laptop told me I had a couple more hours before I could go home and prepare for dinner with my parents.

A long day of work meant by the time I left the office it was already dark outside. It didn't help that it was December in New York City. The sun set earlier, the temperatures were colder, and people were preparing to celebrate holidays. That made a long day in the office feel even longer. I zipped up my thick, insulated winter coat, pulling it tighter around my neck as I steeled myself to brave the cooler temperature outside.

I left the office and headed to the subway. Thankfully, it took no time to get there because the closest station wasn't too far. Sometimes having a car in New York City was helpful.

Sitting in a traffic jam in the driver's seat wasn't, which was why I didn't have one. When I needed a car, I would rent one.

The familiar smells of the subway greeted me. If someone were to ask me what those smells were, I'd tell them it was a combination of many things and leave it at that. I checked my phone to see what time it was when I reached the platform, somewhat patiently waiting for the train. I had about ninety minutes to get to my parents' home, but I was going to stop by my apartment first. I didn't have to wait long for the train to come into the station, screeching to a halt. The conductor opened the doors, and I quickly stepped inside, making my way toward a vacant seat.

I kept my eyes focused on the window once the train pulled out of the station. As the train moved closer and closer to my destination, I was glad I only had to take one train to get to and from work, making my commute easy. Unless there was some sort of incident that screwed up the trains' schedule. About twenty minutes later, I walked over to a set of doors on the left side of the car. Once the train stopped, I jumped off, not paying attention to all the other people who had followed suit. It took almost no time for me to exit the station and start walking down the street. My normal stroll turned into a fast-paced gait because I wanted to escape the cold and get home. I mentally made a list of things I needed to do, like change my clothes, before I headed out to my parents'. I was caught up in my own world when I felt something brush up against me, causing me to jump back.

"Sorry," I said as I realized I had bumped into someone who was walking in the opposite direction. When I heard nothing back, I looked over my shoulder and found a man. The way the streetlights bounced off of his face hid some of his features, but exaggerated others, painting a sinister picture.

"Watch yourself," was all he said. His voice was rough, like how I imagined someone with vocal cords wrapped in sandpaper would sound.

I didn't give him a chance to say or do anything else. I started walking backward down the street, trying my best to keep him in view, in case he tried to do something. Instead, he continued in the opposite direction, not once bothering to turn around to give me a second look. Alarms went off in my head and I became more aware that there weren't any people nearby.

I switched back around as I reached into my purse to grab my keys and my phone, hoping the former was enough of a weapon to buy me time in case I needed to get away. I walked even faster down the street, not caring how silly I looked because I knew I had to get home.

When I could see my building, I said a silent prayer, thankful that I was almost home, and I was pretty sure that the man hadn't followed me. When I crossed the threshold into my apartment building, I breathed a sigh of relief. I was safely in my lobby where there were other people wandering about, and the warmth from the heated building wrapped around me like I had just taken a sip of hot chocolate on a cold winter day.

I made it up to my apartment in record time and whipped off the coat and blazer. A quick call out to see if Ellie Winters, my roommate and best friend, was home confirmed she wasn't. It took longer than normal to unwrap the bun I had placed my hair in that morning, but once the pins were on the table, I could feel the tension easing from my head. But it soon came back with a vengeance when I replayed the scene that had unfolded with my father earlier.

If I knew my father as well as I thought I did, I knew something had to be wrong. Throughout my life, he had been this pillar of strength, never one to sway much in any circumstance. If anyone had a problem and wanted help to solve it, he was there to lend a hand. There wasn't a time I could think of that I'd ever seen him rattled until today. Although he tried to put on a brave face, it did little to prevent his actual feelings from showing through the cracks.

I somewhat dreaded dinner at my parents' house tonight, although it had been a while since we'd had dinner together, just the three of us. If I had to be honest with myself, that was something I missed, but with being so busy it had become a lower priority. I was still feeling weird about the encounter with the strange man and all I wanted to do was put on my pj's and go to bed. But I vowed there was no way I was going to do that. I needed to find out what was going on with Dad. Before I got too lost in thought, my phone chimed, and I placed the creepy incident behind me.

Ellie: *Do you want to go to a gala with me?*

I closed my eyes and groaned before my fingers flew across my keyboard.

Me: *You know how I feel about those types of things, El.*

Ellie: *I think you'll like this one. It's a fundraiser for Project Adoption.*

Project Adoption was a nonprofit created to support the rescue of cats, dogs, and other animals, and to help them find their forever homes. Now I had another reason to go. Besides, Ellie would have dangled my not going over my head for the rest of my life. Ellie's love for animals was one reason her parents supported Project Adoption, so I knew she was dying to go.

Me: *Fine. I'll go.*

Ellie: *Awesome! We can even go dress shopping.*

Me: *I might have something here, but I'll never turn down the excuse to go shopping. Would Thursday work for you?*

Ellie: *Yes, it would. I'm so excited!*

I put my phone in my pocket, determined to finish getting ready for dinner at my parents.

"Dinner was superb as usual, Mom." I leaned back in my chair, debating whether or not it would be proper to loosen the belt I had on. It might not be out in public, but hell, I was home anyway.

"Thanks, dear. I'm glad you liked it." The grin she gave me didn't quite reach her eyes, reaffirming my belief that something was wrong. My mother and I were very open with each other when it came to a multitude of things, and I knew when something was up. Or so I thought. My mom and I shared the same pale skin and long, dark brown hair. I also inherited her thin, fit body type and we shared a love of fitness.

"Anais is right. You really outdid yourself tonight. Thanks, honey." The roasted chicken, broccoli, and crispy potatoes hit all the right spots when it came to a wonderful, comforting meal.

Mom's gaze turned to my father, and she beamed.

Although my parents had enough money to hire people to help them around the house, my mom enjoyed cooking.

Heck, sometimes we would cook together, which had always been fun.

"Anais, can we talk for a moment?"

Dad's words stopped my thoughts. I nodded my head and sat back. "Thanks for dinner, Mom."

"You're welcome. Why don't we take this to the living room?"

"That's a good idea, Ilaria. I'll put the dishes in the sink and then I'll join you in there."

"I can help."

"Don't worry about it. Go relax with your mom while I do this." Dad stood up first and walked over to Mom and rested a hand on her shoulder. He held his hand out and she placed her hand in his and they both stood up. I stood up as well and my mom and I walked together into the living room as Dad was taking the dirty dishes into the kitchen.

I almost asked Mom what was going on, but it was clear that this was something they wanted to tell me together. After we sat down on the couch, Mom reached over and squeezed my hand, telepathically telling me that things were going to be okay. That made me feel worse.

Dad soon joined us and sat next to Mom. He glanced at me but said nothing.

"What is going on? Are you both okay? Is someone sick?"

Mom nodded her head as Dad said, "We're both fine and no one is sick. It's related to work."

I could have fallen back on the couch as relief came over me at the news that no one was sick. Dread trickled in at what he could possibly want to talk to me about regarding work. There was no way he was retiring yet because we'd talked about that briefly earlier this year. I was somewhat shocked he didn't want to talk about this in his office, a place with which I was all too familiar. I remembered being allowed to play on the floor in front of his desk while he spoke on the phone with a client. Then once he'd finished with his calls, he would pull me into his lap and tell me about what he was doing and how he was helping communicate their company's vision with the world. I would say that, without a doubt, he inspired me to go into the field, and I hoped one day when he retired, I would be next in line to run Monroe Media Agency.

"Dad, you're making me nervous. What's up?"

He took a deep breath, and I waited. The weariness I had seen in his eyes earlier that day returned, causing my stomach to shift. Was I even ready to hear what he had to say? If it had something to do with work, was he going to fire me?

"Kiddo, you know how much I appreciate everything you do at Monroe. I don't know where we would be without you and the work you've done over the last five years."

I'm getting fired. I said nothing, but I knew he must have interpreted the look I was giving him correctly: rip off the Band-Aid and tell me what this is all about. I was scared shitless.

It took a second for me to calm my anxieties down when I told myself that he had no reason to fire me. I had done nothing to warrant losing my job. Another idea floated into my mind that shook me even harder: Was Monroe Media Agency going under?

He sighed and Mom said, "Monroe Media Agency isn't doing well."

"What do you mean not doing well?" This was worse than me getting fired.

This time Dad spoke up. "We are losing a lot of money. In fact, it's been happening for a while."

This was the last thing I'd expected my father to say. "Does anyone else know about this?"

He ran a hand through his hair. "A few people do. We kept it secret because we thought we might turn it around quickly, but business hasn't picked up."

I nodded, wrapping my head around what he was saying. "Is there anything I can do to help? Recruit more clients?"

My father reached across my mother and patted my knee, before pulling Mom's hand into his. "You've been doing an amazing job. You and the social media team have been doing a phenomenal job and are the one component keeping Monroe Media Agency alive."

"But that's not enough."

He shook his head. "No. It's not enough, unfortunately. A series of poor investments have hurt us financially, but I'm taking full responsibility because everything stops with me. I'm doing my best to save the company, but we wanted to tell you personally. We didn't want you to hear about it through the rumor mill or potentially from someone else. We will give everyone plenty of notice if they need to find new jobs. We know how much this company means to you."

I didn't know I had cried until a tear landed on my hand resting in my lap. Mom grabbed a tissue from the coffee table and handed it to me. I dabbed at my eyes and sniffled.

"Thanks for telling me."

My mom leaned over and pulled me into her arms, enveloping me in her warmth. How I wished I could stay in her arms and have my problems drift away, much like they did when I was a child.

"Your mother knows what's going on with the company, because I never want to lie to her, and she knows I'm trying to fix everything. And I have a couple of things in the works that might pan out, but nothing is concrete."

"Is there any way I can help?"

"Not right now, kiddo, but I'll let you know if things change."

The desire to tell my parents about the encounter with the man who gave me terrible vibes was shoved to the edges of my mind. His words ran through my mind once more and a sense of unease overtook me, but I assumed my father's news was playing a role as well. After all, we had bigger problems to deal with.

I tried to block the thoughts racing through my mind, because I knew if I didn't, I wouldn't be able to stop crying. My father, the man I had always known to be indestructible, was barely hanging on by a thread. We all rose slowly. Dad took a step around my mother and pulled me into his embrace, and it was something I didn't know I'd needed. I appreciated him coming to me with this issue. Not just as one of his employees, but as his daughter. He knew how much the company meant to me and how one of my own goals was to take it over one day once he retired. Now that dream was hanging in the balance. In an attempt to not go down a rabbit hole of emotions, I took that moment to feel the comfort my father's loving arms brought me.

2

ANAIS

"You look tense."

"And that's why I'm here. Well, outside of seeing you." I loosened my coat as I walked farther into Devotional Spa. Ellie had been working at the spa for the last couple of years.

"I'm glad you clarified that comment." Ellie's smirk was ever present, much to my chagrin.

"Are you giving me a massage or what?"

"You won't let me have any fun, huh?" she asked as she stood up. She headed toward the door, and I followed behind her. "You know the drill. I'll see you in my usual room."

"Thanks." I paused. "Also, thanks for letting me come in at the last minute."

"Not a problem. You know I'm here whenever you need me. You sounded pretty upset, and I had no more appointments, so it was fine."

I stopped to look at her. Her long brown hair was pulled back into a low ponytail and mischief was shining in her brown eyes. She was a couple inches shorter than me, even more so because of me wearing heels to work today. "You have no more appointments because you're supposed to be closed."

"Semantics," she said with a shrug. "How about you get ready, and I'll meet you in the other room? Then maybe we can go out for a drink?"

"That sounds heavenly. You are literally an angel."

"Or a devil in disguise," she told me with a snort. "See you in a second." With that, she left me in the changing room. They designed the brightly lit room in neutral colors and had a couple rows of lockers for people to put their stuff in. There were some neatly folded towels set up on a small counter near a row of sinks for patrons to grab if they needed it. I walked to the row of lockers that I usually went to and placed my valuables inside. It didn't take me long to change out of the clothes I was in, put a robe on, and lock my things up. I then headed to the room that Ellie used for most of the sessions we had together.

The lights in the room were more mellow than the ones in the locker room, creating a warmer and more relaxed atmosphere. Light music was playing in the background and I took off my robe and lay down on the massage table. Once I was settled, Ellie knocked on the door and entered the room. She said nothing as she began the massage. My body relaxed almost immediately, and the stressors of the day flowed from my mind. I knew if Ellie would let me, I would stay on this table forever because it would prevent me from having to face any of the issues that I needed to deal with. Work had been taking a toll on me recently because of longer working hours balancing the clients we had and doing my part to recruit new ones. That, plus a lack of sleep and always being on the go was leading to some of the heightened anxiety I was feeling.

"Relax," she said.

That's when I realized I had tensed up once more. I did my best to think of tranquil and peaceful ideas versus the thoughts that had been raging in my mind for the last couple of weeks. The Swedish massage that I normally received, and that Ellie was giving to me now, helped to relieve the tension and stress that I was feeling. The kneading and circular motions that she was performing worked wonders on my back and I felt some of the troubles from work melt away.

It was time I left work at work and focused on relaxing. I might have nodded off because by the time I came to, Ellie was softly tapping me on the shoulder. I squinted briefly and realized she was standing with her feet crossed, leaning on one of the counters. I closed my eyes once more, not really wanting to move from my position.

"You can head down to the sauna if you want to," she said.

I groaned as I moved my muscles a bit. "That felt amazing, but I think I'm ready for that glass of wine."

"Okay, well, I have a few things to finish up here, but they shouldn't take long. I'll meet you out front."

"Sounds good." I opened one eye to watch her leave the room. I sighed, and it took a couple of seconds for me to convince myself that I need to move in order to get what I desired most right then: wine. I extracted my limp body from the table, grabbed my robe, and headed into the locker room to change back into my work clothes.

Reclothed in my brown dress and black heels, I threw my long brown strands into a quick ponytail. I smiled at my reflection in the mirror, because for the first time in a long time, my pale skin glowed while my green eyes had taken on new life after the massage. I snatched my purse off the bench in the locker room, put on my coat, and walked back into the hallway toward the front desk.

Ellie exited out of another room. "Ready?"

"Yup," I said as I fixed the strap of my bag. "I think that massage made me look twenty-nine again."

Ellie chuckled. "It doesn't hurt that you're only thirty. I just need to say goodbye to Jill at the front desk, and we can be on our way. Are you cool with just heading back to the apartment?"

"Do we even have wine in the apartment?" The idea sounded heavenly. I could take off these shoes for a short while and ride in a car versus the subway.

"Now what type of question is that?" Ellie smirked at me and turned her attention back to the front desk. "Do you need anything from me, Jill?"

Jill smiled. "Nope. Everything is wonderful here. I'll lock things up. I'll see you tomorrow."

"See you tomorrow." Ellie walked over to a side door and held it open for me. "I drove today, so the car's parked in the garage."

"I'm so glad you went into massage therapy."

"Is that because it's beneficial for you?" The sly look on Ellie's face told me she was kidding.

"No, because you're so good at it. Well, I guess it's on a selfish level, because I do directly benefit from it."

"I will let Mom and Dad know. Another point in the win column for me," Ellie said. She was alluding to the fact her parents disapproved of her chosen career path, but she wasn't willing to change her profession to fit their desires.

I nodded as we started down the brightly lit hall. The clacking of my heels echoed off the walls and floor, and soon we reached a huge white door at the end of the corridor. Ellie pushed the door open and held it for me as I walked through. It opened into a smaller hallway with two elevators.

Ellie pressed the down button and turned her head to look at me. "When was the last time we hung out?"

I tried to think. "Has it been about a month? Although we've lived together for years, it has been a while since we saw each other because of work or other obligations."

"Whoa," she said. "I can't believe it's been that long."

"Is this why you wanted to invite me to the gala?"

She shook her head. "It was very last minute and I'm only going because my parents can't go."

"Ah, okay."

"Don't sound so enthusiastic about it."

I chuckled at her sarcasm. I wasn't thrilled about going to an event because when it came to the things that Ellie's parents attended, the people were stuck up, but I wanted to help Ellie out if I could. Throwing on a pretty dress and some makeup was fine, but sometimes schmoozing with other people got tiring.

"I have the invitation at home, so I'll show you when we get there. I know this isn't exactly your scene, but I know you have several fancy dresses or like I said we could go shopping. It would be an opportunity for us to hang out."

"I'm shocked you didn't want to bring one of the guys you're dating."

She shrugged. "I probably could. I want to invite you. Because it's way easier than having to ditch somebody at the end of the night."

That got my attention. Ellie never had a problem securing a date, but never did anything serious. I, on the other hand, hadn't dated in at least six months, and preferred it that way. "Don't you usually have an understanding with the people you date?"

"Yes and no. It's complicated."

"Sounds like it." But I didn't prod any further because the elevator had arrived. We stepped inside and waited as it took us to the garage.

Once the door opened, I stepped out and looked around. "I didn't know there was another way to get down here."

"I know many things about this place and this town."

Although she finished her comment with a wink, I knew she wasn't kidding. I had seen her knowledge in action, and it impressed and terrified me. The random things she retained were both useful and scary.

It wasn't long before we were driving down the New York City streets on the way to our apartment. I watched as the glow from the streetlights bounced off the cars crowding the street. Although it was evening, traffic was still pretty heavy in the "City That Never Sleeps." The low, airy, and soothing music that played at the spa served as the soundtrack for the light conversation we were having to pass the time. The ride home was swift, all things considered, and I sighed and closed my eyes when my back hit the soft cushion of our couch.

"Here you go."

I opened one eye and found a glass of wine staring back at me. "Thanks. Is this Merlot?"

"Yes, it is, and don't worry about it. Also, here's the invitation."

I took the thick ivory-colored card out of her hand and read it over. "Pretty invitation and an open bar."

"Happy to be going now? Plus, what else were you going to do on a Friday evening?"

"Bury myself under a blanket on our couch with a pint of ice cream and watch Netflix?"

"Why are you coming out with me then?"

I laughed as she held out her glass to clink with mine and we sat back to enjoy the delicious wine.

3

DAMIEN

"Is this a family intervention?"

I spared my younger brother Gage a glare as he strolled into the room, fifteen minutes late.

"Glad you could make it," his fraternal twin, Broderick, tossed out from next to me.

We were sitting around an enormous table in one of the many conference rooms in a building that had been dubbed "Cross Tower" due to a lot of our operations utilizing space at this location. Broderick and I had arrived on time to this mysterious meeting, while Gage stayed true to his colors and walked in after we were supposed to arrive.

"Happy to see you too, Ric."

I shook my head at his snark and mentally prepared myself for Broderick to snap back because Gage had shortened his name. This was something that always riled Broderick up when they were kids, and it came as no surprise when they sometimes reverted back to it. My eyes drifted toward the door to see if our father had arrived. What was surprising was our father was late and that was unlike him. Maybe he was operating under the assumption Gage was going to be late, as usual, and was wrapping up a few more things before joining us here.

We all shared brown hair, although the twins' hair was a couple of shades lighter than mine and my father's. Dad's hair was becoming more salt and peppery by the year. He and Gage shared the same hazel eyes while Broderick and I inherited our mother's blue eyes. I smoothed down my black tie, which was usually what I wore to work, and turned to look at the door when I heard it open.

"How about you two cut the bullshit before you revert to five-year-olds?" This was a waste of time.

"Good afternoon, boys. Thanks for coming over on such short notice." Dad walked into the conference room, not hearing any part of the conversation that had just happened.

While I watched him close the door, any other thoughts I had vanished. The one that remained had been nagging at me since he summoned us here just a few hours ago: *Why had Dad called us here with no warning?*

"Gage, have a seat," Dad said as he took a seat across from the three of us on the other side of the table. Gage and Dad arrived at their respective chairs at the same time and took a seat with no fanfare.

"Dad, what's up? What's with the urgency to get us here?" I was glad Broderick addressed the elephant in the room first.

Dad said nothing as he straightened his posture.

"The Meyers merger is moving forward."

Relief flooded the room. We had all been pulling our weight to make sure the deal occurred, and finally our efforts had paid off. Of course, all of this would need to be approved by the board of directors but getting Meyers and Company to this point had taken a couple years of hard work. The board had been ready to approve the deal a year ago. Dad had been the CEO of Cross Industries since our grandfather retired and now Broderick, Gage, and I served as senior vice presidents outside of the ventures we took on outside of the parent company.

"And that's another one added to the empire."

Gage wasn't wrong. Our family had done really well over the years after my great-grandfather had started his first company in the 1800s. It eventually became one of the biggest banks in the United States. That helped start what people called the "Cross Empire" in New York City and around the world.

Dad went into more detail about the next steps in the merger over the course of twenty minutes. We spent a couple of minutes talking about other business before Dad pushed his chair back, signaling that we could wrap things up.

Once we were done, Broderick stood up. "Thanks for calling us in for this, Dad."

"I wanted to keep you up to date. After all, this will shift the focus of the end-of-the-year board meeting a bit, but we should have a call with the rest of the team about it. Before you leave, I wanted to remind you three about the holiday bash your mother is putting together in a couple of weeks."

I smirked when I heard Gage groan. I was sure all of us were thinking it, but two of us had enough sense not to make those feelings known. Mom organized an annual holiday bash for New Year's that I didn't think any of us were particularly fond of, but we attended because she wanted us to.

"Okay, you three can leave now."

We got up and headed toward the exit. My brothers left the room first, and just as I was about to trail after, Dad called me back. "Damien?"

I turned around to face my father.

"A moment? And could you shut the door?"

I raised an eyebrow before complying. I placed both hands in my pockets as I walked back over to the conference room table. Dad slid a folder across the table to me, and it landed just out of my reach.

"What's this?" I asked before I leaned across the table and dragged the file toward me with the tips of my fingers. I flipped the cover open and skimmed part of the first page. In it was information about James Monroe, CEO of Monroe Media Agency. I looked at my father for a second and picked up the folder. He and my father shared similar salt-and-pepper hair, but James's hair was shorter. The photo must have been recent because he looked similar to when I last saw him. The next photo in the file was of a good-looking woman around James's age. It took me a second to confirm she was Ilaria Monroe, James's wife. I flipped through more of the pages until I came across a photo of a stunning brunette with bright green eyes, much like James's. Her skin was paler than his and my mind flirted with what her body would look like underneath me. Who was this? I could see the family resemblance, so she had to be their daughter. When I found her name, I looked up at Dad again. I knew he had caught me staring at the photo for too long based on the look on his face.

"This is the information Dave said you asked him for regarding Monroe. I offered to bring it to you."

I had almost forgotten I'd asked Dave, our in-house private investigator, to dig up some more details on Monroe. "I'm having another meeting with James in the next couple of days."

Dad did a double take. "You let him have another chance? Are you turning over a new leaf?"

"Let's just say I'm feeling jollier, given the season, but this will be taken care of as soon as possible." Her bright green eyes were imprinted on my mind. The second photo showed what the first had missed: her slim yet athletic frame. An idea of how I could make sure that I was paid for my generosity started to form because I knew there was no way Monroe could pay me back in time. Having her come to me willingly would be the ultimate payment.

"Are you sure? You seem...distracted." The gleam in his eye told me we both knew who he was talking about: Monroe's daughter.

My father's voice brought me out of the thoughts I was having. "He borrowed the money from me, and he's going to pay it back. If he doesn't, Monroe Media Agency will go under and be gutted and brought into the Cross Empire."

"And there is the Damien that I know."

I nodded at my father as my thoughts faded back to the woman whose photo was imprinted in my mind. This was new because women sailed in and out of my life on a regular basis and I got what I wanted before I got out.

The ringing of my phone broke my concentration on the woman in front of me. I pulled out my phone and recognized the number.

"Dad, I need to take this."

"Sure. I'll see you later."

I waited until he left and then I answered. "Yes?"

"Tate didn't have the money he owed you."

"Finish him."

"You mean—"

"You know what I mean."

"Do you want it to be quick or slow?"

"I trust your judgment. Just make sure it's handled."

I hung up and returned my phone to my pocket before my eyes drifted back to the file on the table. The women in my life had to submit and I could tell that she wouldn't, yet my attention was focused on her. I knew I needed to find out more information about Anais, the woman whose picture was staring back at me.

"Thanks for coming to my office today. I apologize for not being able to make the trek to your office."

I could feel the nervous energy flying off of James in droves. I couldn't blame him. After all, he didn't know what I might say or do that could upend the life he had built.

It was the day after my father had tossed the folder of information about the Monroe family into my lap. According to what Dave had provided in the file and my own deductions, I figured there was no way James Monroe was going to pay back the money he owed in six weeks.

"It wasn't a problem, and no hardship on my end," I said as I sat down in the chair in front of his desk as he did the same with his chair. Although his demeanor highlighted someone who had a lot of confidence, I could sense the nervousness dripping off of him like raindrops in a storm.

"Mr. Cross—"

A knock on a door interrupted us. James rubbed a hand over his face and said, "Come in."

The door opened and in walked the stunning brunette, from the folder. Anais Monroe. Her eyes darted between the two of us.

"Oh, I'm sorry. I didn't know you were busy. Your calendar said you were free."

"This is something that came up last minute," James said.

I nodded along with him because the meeting had just come together, maybe an hour and a half ago.

I took my time studying the beautiful woman in front of me. She wore her brown hair down, cascading in soft waves on her back, and her eyes had finally settled on her father, even though I knew she was well aware of my presence in the room. She wore a white blouse, navy blazer, and dark blue jeans with beige heels. Thoughts of her hourglass shape wearing only those heels slid into my brain before I could stop it. I discreetly adjusted myself and turned my attention back to her.

"Anais, is it anything that needs to be discussed right now?" James asked. "Oh, wait. Let me introduce you to Damien. This is Anais, the head of our social media team and the person who I have the privilege of calling my daughter. Damien is here to talk to me about a few business things."

I stood up from the chair and leaned over to shake her hand. Her palm was warm and soft, but the handshake she gave me was firm and sent a slight jolt to my cock. I could tell she felt the same, because her eyes lingered at our hands for a second too long before she pulled away and turned back toward her father.

"No, Dad. It can wait, and I'm sorry for interrupting. Nice meeting you, Damien."

"It was nice to meet you too," I replied automatically. *And it won't be the last time.*

4

ANAIS

I hadn't been to one of these events in a while. The urge to run in the other direction was real as Ellie and I walked through the doors of the Olympus Hotel. Our heels clacked along the floor before we both paused, trying to get our bearings, because it seemed as if we'd entered another dimension. The owners designed the hotel in a sophisticated, regal way with reds and golds displayed throughout. The intimidation I felt as a result of attending such a high-profile event with high-profile people crept in.

I thought I had quietly sucked in a deep breath, but the glance Ellie threw me proved otherwise.

"You okay?" she asked, leaning over to whisper in my ear.

"Yeah, I'm fine."

"Are you sure?"

All I did was nod my head. The urge to explain my worries and fears to her was there, but this was neither the time nor the place.

"You know, I was shocked you wore red, but I'm loving this gown."

The dark red gown had been sitting in my closet for well over a year, because I didn't have anywhere to wear it. The split down my right leg made it easier for me to walk in the black strappy heels I had also owned for a year or two and barely worn. I finished my look by throwing my hair into a French twist on the top of my head and applying a dark red lipstick to match the dress. Although my shopping excursion with Ellie hadn't been successful for me, she looked stunning in her new dark green V-neck gown with spaghetti straps and an open back. She wore her dark brown hair down over her shoulders.

"Thanks. Honestly, I should have worn black. That would have fit my mood better tonight."

"Hush," Ellie said. "This'll be over before you know it."

"Will it, though?"

"May I help you?" A woman dressed in a black suit and black shirt greeted us.

"We're here for the Project Adoption gala."

When Ellie finished her sentence, the woman in front of us lit up. "Oh, it's right down this hall and to your left. May I check your coats?"

"That would be great." We both took off our coats and handed them to the attendant, who then took them to coat check. She returned to give us our tickets.

"Thank you so much," I said as Ellie gave the woman a smile and nod before we trekked down the hall. "I hope we don't have to stay here too long. These heels are going to rob me of circulation in my feet."

"But they're beautiful."

"That's true," I said, glancing down to admire the shoes as we continued down the hall. It didn't take long for us to figure out which room we were in based on the sign sitting on a stand outside the door. Moments later, Ellie and I were standing off to the side, opposite the entrance, sipping on glasses of wine and taking in the scenery in front of us.

"You know, I think people watching is my favorite sport."

"I think it's mine too," I replied as I let my eyes float around the room. It was then that I looked back toward the entrance and a gasp fell from my lips.

"Hey, what's wrong with—"

I didn't hear the rest of Ellie's question. That was because my eyes settled on a man who struck both excitement and fear into me at the same time. I couldn't stop the shiver that flowed through my body once his blue eyes landed on mine. The way they perused my body made me think he was undressing me in his mind, similar to the vibe I had gotten when we'd met in Dad's office. I offered Damien the same treatment back as I stared at him from the top of his flawlessly styled brown hair to his shoes that looked barely worn. The standard black tuxedo reminded me of the suit he had worn to my office, but instead of wearing a black tie, he switched it out for a bow tie. It fit his body to perfection, and I would bet my paycheck it was custom made. Well, that bet wouldn't be worth too much, seeing as I didn't know how long I would have one.

"Hey, Anais—"

Out of the corner of my eye, I could see Ellie go from staring at me to the tall, dark, and handsome man standing across the room.

"Earth to Anais. Come back down from the clouds."

The words she whispered caught my attention. "Wait, what?"

"You've seemed to have caught Damien Cross's eye. Word on the street says that is both a blessing and a curse."

"Can you give me an overview here?"

"Mr. Tall, Dark, and Handsome over there is as dangerous as he is good-looking. Not to mention he and his family are richer than Bill Gates. I've heard stories about some of his exploits and not just the ones that were mentioned in the tabloids. Are you even listening to me?"

"Nope," I said. At least I was being honest. "We've met before. Briefly."

"And you didn't tell me?" Ellie's question came out as a harsh whisper, but I could hear the shock and knew she would tell me off later.

"I didn't think it was a big deal."

"I didn't think it was a big deal," she mumbled under her breath, lightly mocking me.

I snorted in return, used to this behavior from her. I saw movement out of the corner of my eye and a glance at Ellie forced me to break eye contact with Damien.

She took a deep breath and said, "We need to talk later." Ellie's eyes shifted between us rapidly. "Oh, yeah, we definitely need to talk later."

I looked back in Damien's direction and saw he was still looking at me. Before anyone could do anything, a voice broke through the chatter in the crowd and asked if everyone could take their seats because the program was about to begin. Ellie and I sat down, and I was disappointed we weren't sitting at the same table as Damien, but there was nothing that could be done about that. It wasn't surprising he was seated at a table near the front and we were seated a couple of rows back. The table and the room were decorated to resemble an A-list event, playing off the reds and golds that were a part of the décor of the hotel. Project Adoption made sure to include pets in their theme. Each name card included a picture of an animal on it. I smiled at the dog on mine.

The MC of the night caught my attention when he walked up to the microphone and announced what we would be seeing this evening to support Project Adoption. He kept the gala interesting and lively, removing some of the hesitation I had about attending the event in the first place. About an hour into the gala and during a pause in the musical numbers, speeches, and auctions on stage, I leaned over to Ellie and whispered, "I'm going to go to the ladies' room."

She nodded, and I grabbed my purse and walked out of the large hall. It took me a moment to figure out where the bathrooms were, but once I spotted them, I walked as fast as my heels would let me. Thankfully, I made sure my gown wouldn't take too much time or effort for me to use the bathroom. Within a few minutes, I was drying off my hands, ready to head back into the gala. I opened the door and stepped outside.

"Nice to see you here."

I whipped around to find out where the rich timbre had come from. I was startled to find Mr. Tall, Dark, and Handsome standing just a couple of feet away. His blue eyes shone even brighter now than they had when we'd met in my father's office a few days ago. I looked to see if anyone was around before my gaze landed back on him. I forgot to breathe for a second as I examined him without trying to make it too obvious. I couldn't deny that he looked good.

"What are you doing here?" I asked.

He said nothing but motioned for me to take a step closer.

When I did, he put his hand on my lower back and led me toward a row of windows overlooking the entire city. His scent, a woodsy and spicy fragrance with a hint of something floral, crept into my nose, embraced, and consumed me. Yet there was still a sense of danger that I couldn't pinpoint. I knew I wouldn't be able to smell this aroma again without thinking of him. When he stopped walking, I took a step back, even though I craved the warmth his touch brought on my bare skin. It felt very intimate for someone I barely knew.

"I can't attend an event to support animals? I do like them, and I assume you do too."

"Sure you can, but that doesn't require you to stop me from getting where I want to go. Excuse me."

I tried to remain as polite as possible as I took a step to the left to get around Damien, but he blocked my path. I moved to the right and he blocked me again.

"Move." My voice was low and menacing. I didn't want to cause a scene and embarrass Ellie and her parents, but I also had no problem doing so to get away from him. "Get the hell out of my way."

"No, and the quicker you realize that no one can tell me what to do, the better."

I rolled my eyes. "What do you want?" I asked.

"I have a proposition for you."

His eyes were stuck on mine. They didn't waver once. The blue orbs turned cold when I talked back to him. Confidence oozed off of him, making me feel intimidated by his presence, but I refused to back down.

"Well?" I asked, waiting for him to proceed.

"I wanted to talk to you about a deal I have with your father."

My eyes narrowed as I tried to figure out what he was getting at. "What type of deal?"

He put both of his hands in his pockets and said, "I'm sure it comes as no surprise to you that Monroe Media Agency is having money troubles."

I could have growled at him because he dared to utter my family business's name and spread information I hated to say was true. I glanced around once more, making sure no one was within hearing distance before I took a step closer. "This deal was the reason why you were at our office?"

"Yes, your father owes me money after I offered to help Monroe Media Agency survive about two months ago. I gave him an opportunity to pay it back, but he couldn't so I extended the deadline. Even with the boost Monroe Media Agency has received recently, it would take a miracle for him to pay me back everything I loaned him." He paused. "But there's a catch."

"And what is that?"

"Your father has six more weeks to pay back the loan, and based on the meeting I had with him and my research, that will not happen." He licked his lips and continued, "But I have one extra provision I want to include in this deal that, if it happens, would pay off his debt."

"Oh, really? And what is that?"

"You."

I took a step back as my glare became more prominent. "Excuse me? What do you mean me?"

It was clear who was running the show here. One side of his lips curved upward. "I want you."

My blood turned as cold as his eyes. "Can you repeat that?"

He took a step forward, entering my personal bubble once more. "I rarely repeat myself, but I'll make the exception just this one time. I want you."

I couldn't stop the feeling that he had become my worst enemy.

5
ANAIS

"I heard you, but I must be stuck in another dimension because I'm not comprehending it. What do you want with me?"

He took a step closer and said, "You will be mine for thirty days. Whatever I say goes." He leaned even closer and I got another whiff of his cologne.

I didn't want to admit it, but the scent spoke to me like how the smell of a decadent cake would make your mouth water. Yet his words and the intimidation he swung around like a sword made anything that could have been wet dry up like the Sahara.

"I'll even be generous and give you a couple days to think it over."

"Are you saying you want to have sex with me in exchange for paying off my father's debt?" The question flew out of my mouth and I didn't care. It didn't matter that it drew attention to us and could cause a scene.

"Those were your words, Anais. Not mine."

No.

No way.

No way in hell.

He didn't deny my interpretation of his proposal. It had always been hard for me to keep my feelings from showing on my face, but I succeeded and my face remained neutral. Inside, I was mortified at the words that had flown out of my mouth, but I was also too enraged to let that feeling take over. My body tensed up as I subconsciously tried to control the heat that was threatening to take over my face. Who did he think I was?

What further pissed me off was the fact that I could see a smile tugging at his lips. I was itching to slap him but thought better of it. "How do I know you're telling the truth?"

"I don't appreciate my honesty being called into question. You and I both know I'm not lying, but I'm happy to show you proof." He pulled out his cell phone and showed me a screenshot of what looked like a contract that my father had signed. "Now, as I said, this will be for thirty days. You will do anything I ask. If I were to tell you to run up and down Seventh Avenue naked, the only question you may ask me is for how long. If I said to stop in my office for a quick fuck, then you'll do it, without hesitation."

His comment left me speechless, unable to comprehend how this man could be this much of an asshole. My lips trembled, not with tears, but frustration and anger. Not once throughout our whole interaction had his demeanor changed. Even as he reached into his suit jacket pocket, the same calm and arrogant man who approached me was still present. It was like the demands he gave were just an everyday transaction. Hell, maybe to him they were.

On the other hand, my stomach felt as if it were racing to my chest, demanding to be let out of the prison it was in. Funny enough, based on what he said, I felt as if I was about to be thrown into one. He pulled out what looked to be a cream-colored business card and handed it to me.

"And if I don't agree to this...arrangement?" I glanced down at the card and realized that it was indeed his business card with a number scrawled onto the back.

"Your father needs to pay me in full in six weeks. And if he doesn't...well. I don't think you want to find out what happens if he doesn't. I look forward to hearing your answer."

I was sure he heard me gulp after his statement as I tried my best to not avert my gaze from his. I could handle clients like Edward all day, defusing tension as I went, but this was different. He was different and he was demanding so much more of me. He wanted my body, my soul, and my dignity.

The smirk that appeared on his face before he turned to walk away sent a small shudder through me. *Is this even legal? But even if I protest it, will I get anywhere with it?* He knew he had me between a rock and a hard place, which, if I was being frank, was exactly where he wanted me...in more ways than one. Thoughts raced through my head as I tried to process the conversation we had shared. Was it even worth me returning to the gala? My mind was going to be elsewhere anyway.

No, I would head back in, sit down next to Ellie, and make it through this evening. I would not let him see that he had gotten to me. When we got back to our apartment, I needed to do my research on Damien Cross. I didn't want to bring Ellie into this, but I knew her vast knowledge of people in this city would be helpful. Right now, I needed all the help I could get.

I locked my knees for a second to avoid sinking to the ground. There was no way I was going to faint if I had any control over it. I took a deep breath and marched back toward the gala with my back straight and my head held high. I didn't know who might be watching and I wanted to show that what had happened hadn't affected me. Ellie threw a glance in my direction when I sat back down in my seat but said nothing. Not that she needed to anyway, because I knew what the question would be: *Where were you?*

∽

"Well, that wasn't so bad after all," I said as Ellie and I walked outside of the Olympus Hotel. I shivered briefly when the cold air hit my face and pulled my coat's collar tighter around my neck. After sitting inside of a warm room for a couple of hours, my body was not ready for the cold, blistering wind.

"Yeah, it was fantastic. Even the fifteen minutes that you missed when you went to the bathroom."

Most things didn't get past Ellie and I shouldn't have expected anything different here. I debated summarizing my encounter with Damien but paused, because of course he was standing a few feet away.

"He would arrive in a limo," Ellie whispered as we watched the driver walk around the back of the car and open the door closest to Damien. Damien paused and looked over his shoulder. Our eyes met once more and I swallowed hard, wondering what he might do next. All of that was for naught because he gave me a small nod and got into the limousine. His driver shut the door and walked around the car again before getting into the driver's seat.

"What's going on? What's up with him staring you down? This is at least the second time that has happened tonight," Ellie whispered.

I heard her, but didn't respond right away. Instead, I was spellbound by the menacing aura of the man who had thrown this challenge at my feet. It was then that I realized I hadn't said anything in a while.

"I'm not even sure." I knew that there was some hesitation in my voice based on the side-eye Ellie gave me. I could only admit to myself that I was lying. I knew exactly what was up with Damien Cross.

"Well, good thing we live together so we have plenty of time to chat about this."

"Yeah. Let's do that."

"Ma'am?"

We both turned toward the unfamiliar voice. An attendant from the hotel was standing a few feet away, trying to help with traffic and to make sure that the guests left the hotel safely.

"Can I get you two a taxi?"

"Yes, please. That would be great," Ellie answered for the both of us. Before you could snap your fingers, a taxi pulled up and both Ellie and I were sitting inside on our way back to our apartment.

I was waiting for Ellie to bring up tonight's events on the ride home, but she didn't. It, for some reason, made me nervous. Usually, she had no problem talking my ear off about things that were happening in either of our lives, so her silence was odd. When we arrived, Ellie stopped to grab the mail out of our mailbox in the lobby while I summoned the elevator so that it would be there when she made her way over to me. The elevator reached the lobby before Ellie reached me, so I stepped inside and held the doors open.

"Ellie!"

"Coming! I'm coming!"

Once she was on, I moved my arm away and watched the doors close. "Would it be weird if I took these shoes off right now?"

"A little. We are thirty seconds from our front door."

She was right and once my feet hit the door, I snatched the heels off and sighed. My feet on the rug near our front door felt heavenly.

Our apartment wasn't much, but it was home. It was on the smaller end for two people, but we made it work. It had a living room, kitchen, one bathroom that Ellie and I shared, and two small bedrooms. We could afford to upgrade to a place that was a smidge bigger, but we enjoyed the convenience of having the subway and buses nearby.

"I'm going to change and then we can chat."

"Sounds good. I'll do the same and make popcorn so we have something to snack on. There's never enough food at those things."

With that, I went to my room and changed out of the beautiful gown that I wore this evening. Then, I grabbed some makeup wipes and headed over to my mirror to remove my makeup. As I was wiping my face, I found myself staring in the mirror, still shaken by the demand Damien had made.

Although he had presented the deal as if I had a choice, something deep down in my heart told me I didn't have one. It was either be his for thirty days or have Monroe Media Agency go under and deal with those ramifications. The cold, wet cloth did little to soothe the irritation that was growing within me as I tried to find a way out of the predicament that I was in. The audacity he had to even suggest a thing showed how much of an asshole he was.

"Anais?" Ellie called through the door.

"Ah, yeah?" I looked down at my hand and found that I had stopped rubbing the wipe across my skin and had crumpled it in my fist without even noticing.

"Popcorn is ready."

"I'll be out in a minute." That was the second lie that I told tonight.

I walked into our joint bathroom across the hall with another wipe and did my best to remove as much of the makeup as I could without causing my skin to flare up. I then washed my face, mostly in an attempt to cleanse it, but I hoped that it would cool down the rage that was coursing through my body.

When I finished drying off, I walked over to my dresser and took out the pins holding my hair in place. The tension that was released from my scalp brought some relief as I threw my hair up into a messy ponytail. My hoodie and sweatpants marked the start of what should have been a quiet night, but the thoughts flying through my mind would make that anything but. One quick glance in the mirror proved that this was as good as it was going to get, and I walked out of my bedroom and moved toward the living room. Just before I entered, I stopped in the doorway. I was hit with how much Monroe Media Agency meant to the people who worked there and the services that we provided to our clients all around the world. Now, all of that might go up in smoke unless I did this.

"Anais?"

Ellie's voice caused the thoughts in my mind to stop turning. I looked at her and said, "Ah, I'm sorry. What's up?"

"I asked if you wanted water or wine. Is everything all right? You looked like you were elsewhere."

"Yeah, I'm fine. I have a lot on my mind," I said, turning toward the kitchen.

"Does that include Damien Cross?"

I hesitated for a moment before continuing on my way. Just mentioning his name was enough to increase the edginess that I was already feeling. I grabbed the popcorn that Ellie made and put a couple of pieces into my mouth.

"Aha!" she exclaimed. "I knew it."

"Yeah, but not for the reason you're thinking," I mumbled.

"What was that?"

"Nothing."

"So, what was up with tonight? Seemed that anytime you were in his sight, his eyes were glued to you."

I didn't know how much about my brief history with Damien I should tell Ellie. Would she somehow get dragged into this? I was willing to bet he was petty enough to do it. It took me a moment for me to think of what I deemed safe enough to tell her. "So, I met Damien when he came into our office this week. He had a meeting with my dad."

"Oh, is Monroe Media Agency gonna be working for the ever-growing 'Cross Empire'?"

"Something like that. I'm not sure because I wasn't in the

meeting. My dad forgot to block out his calendar for that time, so I ended up interrupting them."

"Hmm, and now he can't seem to take his eyes off of you whenever you're near."

I scoffed. "Well, I wouldn't say that. I highly doubt he's interested in me." *Interested in humiliating me? Yes. Interested in dating me? Ha. No.*

"Of course you wouldn't, but you never do. That's part of the reason you've been single for so long." She leaned over and snatched some popcorn from the bowl while I rolled my eyes.

"I'm single by choice, thank you very much."

"Oh, I think you just bury yourself in work to avoid having to deal with dating. It gives you an excuse not to."

She was right, in part. I had been working longer hours, but it wasn't so I didn't have to date. I buried myself in work so that I could do my part to make sure that the company succeeded. I thrived on helping our clients market their businesses. Monroe Media Agency had a lot of blood, sweat, and tears from my father built into its foundation and once I graduated from college and joined the company, I put in my fair share of them as well.

"That's ridiculous. I've been on dates recently." This was a silly disagreement to be having, but I let it continue because it stopped us from having to talk about Damien.

"Oh, really? When's the last time you went on a date?" She folded her arms and leaned back on the kitchen counter.

"Maybe six months ago?"

"Exactly."

I stopped myself from rolling my eyes again because I had proved her point.

"Now you've caught Damien's attention and you need to make a decision about what you're gonna do about it."

She wasn't wrong. "I'm not sure what I'm going to do, but since you know everything there is to know about everyone, why don't you tell me more about Damien?" I couldn't avoid it anymore. It was time to learn more about the man who had gone from a very attractive businessman to my adversary in less than a week.

Ellie paused. "Before I begin, you might want to grab a drink and follow me to the living room because what I'm about to tell you will be plenty of entertainment for us. Who needs a movie?"

I shook my head and followed Ellie after I grabbed a glass of Merlot and the bowl of popcorn. She settled down on the couch and looked at me.

"I will fully admit, some of what I know about Damien and his family is hearsay, but I'll start with the facts. Damien is the oldest of three boys who were born to Martin and Selena Cross. His brothers are named Broderick and Gage and they are twins. I believe they got their start generations ago and have built their business and power ever since. The Cross family have amassed a fortune through their different business ventures as far as I know."

"Oh, yeah?" I said and stuffed my mouth full of popcorn. I cradled the glass of wine and said, "I might need something a little stronger to deal with this conversation."

"I don't blame you." She paused and threw a couple of pieces of popcorn into her mouth.

"Thanks for understanding," I said, bringing the glass to my lips. I was shocked I could take a sip given how much my mind was racing and my hand was trembling. Ellie didn't act like she noticed, though.

"Damien is a pretty well-known playboy. Most women he's with don't last for more than a month or two tops based on what the gossip blogs say. There have been rumors that he either goes to their place to have sex or he has his driver pick them up and drop them off back home the same night. Sleeping over at his place is a big no-no. I learned that from a source that leaked it to the tabloids. There are also rumors that he might be a co-owner of Elevate."

I choked on my wine. It took everything in me to hold it in and not splatter the contents of my mouth all over everything in front of me. Elevate was one of the hottest nightclubs in New York City. It had a dance club and bar on the main floor and was rumored to be a sex club in the basement.

"Are you all right?" Ellie hit my back as she tried to clear my throat.

I got the remaining wine down and nodded. "Yep. I'm fine." A small tear formed in the corner of one eye. I wondered if it was from the choking or the rabbit hole my thoughts were determined to jump down. I wasn't a virgin by any means, but I was worried about what Damien might do to me.

Ellie looked over at me once more before she continued, "I preface this by saying, once again, this is all rumors as I have personally never interacted with him, but it wouldn't be a bad idea for you to let loose a little bit, you know? You haven't gotten laid in months so what would be so wrong with having some fun with him? Chances are it won't last long anyway."

"Uh-huh." That made sense. And the thirty-day time limit

he put on our arrangement fit the playboy description Ellie gave him.

"That's what I heard. I wouldn't even call it dating him if I had to be honest. When the women he's fucking become addicted to him, he cuts them loose. And when he's done, he's done. He doesn't do relationships. If he gets tired of you, that's it."

I nodded as an idea started forming in my head. I could annoy him to the point that he would get over me and let me go. Based on my brief interactions with him, I bet that wouldn't be too difficult. He thrived on being in control of everything and everyone, and although there was no way that was happening here, maybe I wouldn't even have to make it the full thirty days.

I shook my head. Had I already decided that this was what I was going to do? Well, technically I guess Damien made it up for me because I didn't have much of a choice to begin with outside of going to maybe the police, who would probably laugh me out of the precinct. But with those barriers removed, would I go to the authorities? Conflicting feelings ran through me, so I used my conversation with Ellie to force myself to think about something else.

"So, tell me more about Elevate."

Ellie stretched and said, "Well, there's not much to tell."

"What do you mean there isn't much to tell?"

"It's extremely exclusive. Not much has gotten out about it. They force everyone to sign forms stating that they won't reveal what happens downstairs. It's hard to get on the guest list to just party on the main floor. Trust me, I've tried."

"That makes sense," I said. "I mean, they're probably trying to protect the identities of whoever is attending."

"Right. If I had to make a guess, I would say the club probably caters to New York City's elite based on the lack of information about the place and who the Crosses associate with. Now, I mean this with all the love and care in the world, and I don't mean to offend, but I'm not sure why Damien would be so laser-focused on you. Yes, you're stunning with a kick-ass personality and have a million and a half great things going for you. But the fact that you're in his crosshairs is a huge deal. I don't know if I would call it a good thing or a bad thing."

I licked my lips as my hand made its way to my temple to gently rub it. "I wouldn't say that he is laser-focused on me. We met recently and saw each other at the gala tonight. That's it."

"Oh, really?" Ellie asked. "Then why do you have his business card?"

"Wait, how did you know I have his card? And it isn't uncommon for me to have business cards."

Ellie held out a small cream-colored piece of paper. "I don't think you closed your clutch tightly because this fell out." She flipped the card around. "It has a number scribbled on the back of it that I would bet money is his personal phone number."

"Give that to me." I snatched the card out of her hand.

"Anais, you can try to explain this away, but I know what I saw and what this looks like."

"We just met once and he's doing some business with my father and—"

"Anais, I'm not judging you. I'm all for you getting some, but if you play with the devil, you will get burned." She ran a hand through her long brown hair before she continued,

"Don't forget that you two don't run in the same circles. He has the ability to do more than we could ever dream of. He has enough money to protect you from everything yet destroy you with a flick of his finger."

I knew she was one hundred percent telling the truth about that.

6
ANAIS

Later that night, I was lying in bed and the things that Ellie said made the hairs on the back of my neck stand up. The kicker about the whole thing was that she was right about what Damien wanted with me. Sure, there were easier ways for him to find someone who would be at his every beck and call, so why me? I tried not to jump to conclusions because I knew I would spend my time overthinking instead of figuring out how to get out of this mess.

I knew that beyond any doubt I needed to talk to my father. Why had he decided to go to Damien, of all people, instead of going to a bank and asking for a loan? Hell, couldn't he do that now and use it to pay off Damien? If he could have, why didn't he do it already?

That made me sit straight up in bed. What had kept my father from trying to get a loan from a bank versus going to this man who had just threatened to take his daughter for his own pleasure? These questions caused a surge of energy to run through my body and motivated me to pull myself together in order to get ready for work. It didn't take me long to get it together because I had my weekday morning routine down to a science and I knew exactly how much time I could waste before I had to jump in the shower.

When I was done, I walked into the hallway and found Ellie's door closed. She probably had an early day today and had already left for work. Once I had my coat on, I grabbed my purse and keys and headed out the door. As I waited for the elevator, I dug around in my purse and found my headphones. They would allow me to ignore the world for a bit as I rode the train to work.

It didn't take long for me to reach my office and I dashed through the lobby and went up to my floor on the elevator. A quick check of the time told me that I wasn't late, yet I was still anxious. By the time I reached my desk, I let out a huge sigh. My anxiety was because of Damien's proposal and the questions I wanted to ask my father, since that seemed to be the only thing I could think about. I looked through my doorway, which gave me the perfect angle to see my dad's office. Based on the lack of lights on in his office, Dad still hadn't made it in.

"That's odd," I mumbled as I walked around to sit at my desk. I flipped open my laptop to wake it up. I pulled out my phone and sent a quick text to my father.

Me: *Dad, are you coming into the office today?*

I set my phone down and began reading the emails that had accumulated after I left the office yesterday. I had been so engrossed in what I was reading, I hadn't realized that thirty minutes had flown by until one of my subordinates, Jake, was standing outside my door.

"Sorry, I got caught up reading emails. What's up?"

"FYI, Edward is probably going to call you in a few minutes. Every time I give him an explanation of why a post wasn't performing well, he listens to me and then says that he has to speak to you."

I sighed and closed my eyes. "That's fine. Thanks for giving me a heads-up."

"Don't mention it." Jake lingered for a second longer before he left. I knew that at any moment Edward would call me, and it was pointless trying to work on something new when I was just going to get interrupted. So, I picked up my phone to check to see if Dad had texted me back. I confirmed he had, and I turned my phone on vibrate before I read his message.

Dad: *Yes, I'll be in the office shortly. Had a meeting this morning, probably forgot to mark it down on my calendar.*

A quick search proved that he had indeed forgotten to mark it down. To be honest, this wasn't shocking given the number of things he was balancing on a regular basis.

Me: *Dad, you really need a secretary or an assistant.*

I added a smiley face at the end of the text message and pressed send when a knock on the door startled me. When I looked up, I saw the woman I had passed at the front desk this morning holding a bouquet of pink orchids.

"Anais?"

I nodded.

"These are for you."

I hesitated before I stood up and walked over to take the flowers. "Thanks so much for bringing these up," I said.

"Not a problem. Looks like someone wanted you to know that they were thinking about you."

"Yeah, I guess so," I said as I stared at the flowers. "Thanks again."

With a smile, she left, and I closed my office door.

My phone buzzed before I could inspect the flowers further.

Dad: *I should be in the office in a couple of minutes. I'm about a block away.*

Me: *Sounds good. I want to chat with you about the money thing.*

I knew the flowers had to have been from him, unless it was some secret admirer that was coming out of the woodwork. With that, I placed my phone down on the desk and found the note card that came with the arrangement.

Anais,

Looking forward to hearing your decision.

Damien

The growl that left my lips shocked me. His arrogance jumped off the small piece of paper, as if he knew the answer that I was going to give. My thoughts were interrupted again by the buzzing of my phone. Apparently, I was popular today. I picked it up. I found a message from a number I didn't recognize, and the words caused a small amount of bile to rise in my throat.

Unknown Number: *Did you get the flowers?*

Me: *Damien?*

Damien: *Would someone else be sending you flowers?*

My head jerked back involuntarily when I read his response. The possessiveness rolled off his words in droves. Who the hell did he think he was? I didn't owe him an explanation, period.

Me: *How did you get this number? And I don't owe you any explanation about anything going on in my life.*

He didn't reply right away, and I figured either he was doing it on purpose, or he might have gotten pulled into a meeting. I stared my phone down for a few more seconds before looking at my office phone. *Wasn't Edward supposed to call me?* A knock on the door removed that thought from my mind.

"Come in!"

Dad opened the door and stepped inside, closing it behind him. "Hey sweetheart, do you want to talk? I have a few minutes before my next meeting."

"Dad, I'll cut right to the chase. How much money do you owe Damien Cross?"

"How did you know I borrowed the money from him?"

Shit. I hadn't realized he hadn't told me that he was borrowing money from anyone. "Uh. I put two and two together when you didn't tell me that he was a new client of ours." Thank goodness for my ability to think quickly on my feet.

He didn't respond at first, but he seemed to buy my explanation. He walked over to one of the chairs that I kept in a corner of my office and pulled it closer to my desk before he replied.

"About $270,000."

"Dad!" I exclaimed.

His gaze darted toward the door, probably checking to make sure that no one had heard me through the closed door. "I know, I know."

"$270,000?" I said. I knew I sounded like a parrot, repeating what he had said, but I couldn't help it.

"Sweetheart, I know."

"Are you anywhere near being able to pay that money back? Like, would you be able to get it in six weeks?" I knew the pleading in my words and the uncomfortable nature of this conversation were getting to him because he still hadn't looked at me.

"Potentially."

"What do you mean potentially!" I sounded frantic to my own ears. I paused and said, "I mean I know what *potentially* means, but why aren't you sure? And what happens if you don't?"

"Monroe Media Agency is no more." He stopped and ran a hand across the back of his neck. "We'll have to shut our doors. I'm not sure what your mom and I will do but we'll figure out how to make it work."

"Why didn't you go to the bank and get a loan?"

"Interest rates, and I wasn't sure that they would loan us this amount."

"I've heard some things about Damien Cross, and I don't think he's someone to mess with."

"I know, but I had no choice. No bank was going to loan me that type of money that quick." His eyes made their way around the room before they met mine. "He made me an offer I couldn't refuse. I did it to save this business. To save what you, me, and everyone here worked so hard to achieve, and to give me some more time to fix everything. New companies were springing up and taking our clientele and we needed some more money in order to compete."

I could see tears welling up in his eyes as he ran a hand through his salt-and-pepper hair. I looked down on my desk in order to not start tearing up again myself. Not only had

Damien made my father an offer he couldn't refuse, he had done the same to me.

At the end of the workday, I found myself staring at my phone. Damien had responded hours ago at this point, but I didn't have an urge to read it until now.

Damien: *I have my sources. One more day.*

Reading the words again and again made my lip quiver. Although I was scared there was something else there—a tiny bit of excitement about the unknown? I didn't know if I would call it that either. The fact that I was even considering doing this and not just telling everyone involved to go screw themselves told me a lot about myself. As I was staring into space in the direction of my phone, it lit up alerting me that I had just received a message. It was from Ellie.

Ellie: *You'll never guess what happened.*

Me: *This sounds dangerous and I'm not going to even try to guess what happened.*

Ellie: *Fine. Sometimes I wonder why we're friends. Anyway. You'll never believe this.*

She didn't type for a moment, drawing this out even more.

Ellie: *I just got you and me into Elevate.*

I felt my eyes almost bulge out of my skull.

Me: *You got us into a sex club?*

Ellie: *I got us into the dance club portion. I hope you're ready to party because we are definitely going tonight.*

I sighed and mumbled, "Damnit." I was not prepared for this. Not at all.

7

DAMIEN

"You don't look like you're having much fun. Not that you have much fun to begin with."

I glanced at Broderick and I fought the urge to roll my eyes. "I know how to have fun."

I hadn't intended on coming to Elevate tonight. The twins had insisted, and I didn't give them much of a fight. We had opted to stay in the VIP section of the bar, and I was glad. The sleek black, gray, and gold was a theme across both the bar and the adult club in the basement. The atmosphere of the bar and dance floor could be changed on a dime by switching the music and the lighting, which was one of the reasons we had gone along with this option when the interior designer had suggested it. We knew it made the place look more expensive and that had been the aim when it came to making our money back on the investment. And we did, and then some.

Instead of wandering down to the basement, I stayed up here and nursed the whiskey that had been thrust into my hand when I arrived. Based on where Gage's attention lay, he might have found a woman to take home tonight. He leaned over Broderick and said to me, "Well, pull the stick out of your ass and have some fun."

Broderick shook his head, and I took another sip of my whiskey. Broderick was sitting between us, making it harder to talk one-on-one, not that I was complaining. The music blaring through the speakers didn't help either. Although it was quieter in VIP, it was still difficult to hear.

Both Broderick and I ignored him, and Broderick placed both of his elbows on the back of the couch we were lounging on. My brothers and I had always wanted to go in on a project together but could never agree on anything until we saw that this space was available. Elevate was born and it had been a tremendous success. The grand opening was a couple of years ago, and nothing had stopped the steady stream of people coming through its doors. We made it a point to make both the bar and club somewhat exclusive because we thought that would attract more attention and consumers and it had. Besides, there were well-placed rumors flying around that the three of us co-owned it although no one had proved it.

Gage was right. I did have a stick up my ass because I didn't want to be here and because of a certain brunette that I couldn't shake no matter how much I tried. I spent most of my adult life focusing on work and finding the next company to conquer, but now things felt strange because I couldn't escape my thoughts about her. My quality of work hadn't suffered, however, and I made sure to keep it that way.

There were plenty of women who came in and out of my life. We had our fun, and when it was time to let go, we let go.

I can't remember the last time a woman, especially one who I barely knew, stayed on my mind for this long.

I took another sip of my drink and stood up. Broderick looked over at me and before he could ask, I said, "I'm going to check out the crowd tonight. I'm tired of sitting."

"I'll go with you. I don't want to be stuck next to him."

I looked at Gage and shook my head. He was flirting with a server.

"Come on," Broderick said and together we walked over toward a balcony that overlooked the entire ground floor. It was clear as day that drinks were flowing, and people were dancing and having a good time.

"Excellent investment." Broderick held up his glass and I joined him in a silent cheer before we took another sip. "So what else do you want to take over?"

"What do you mean?" I asked, answering his question with a question.

"Well, you are a mega tycoon, according to the supermarket tabloids." We'd definitely turned the nightlife scene on its head with Elevate in more ways than one. It was then that I spotted her, and my gaze narrowed. "You're one of the most powerful men in New York City. What's next?"

"Same could be said about you and Gage."

"That's not an answer."

"Maybe a media firm."

Broderick took a glimpse at me, his eyes widening before he caught himself and turned back toward the balcony. He was trying to find what had made me say it. "Do you know her?"

"Know who?"

"Good job on being evasive, Damien." Broderick looked

down again over the balcony. "It's the woman in the gold dress, isn't it?" They were making their way across the dance floor and I almost strained my neck in order to get a better look at what she was wearing.

I didn't answer, instead taking another sip of my drink.

"Is there something going on here? Are you fucking her?"

"No." *At least not yet.*

"But you want to."

"That's none of your business."

Broderick snorted. "And that explains why there is a bigger stick up your ass than normal. Maybe you *do* need to fuck her."

"Can you shut up? Or go back to watching what Gage is up to?" His brother didn't need to know that fucking her wasn't out of the realm of possibility given the deal I came up with. I never had to worry about whether I would be able to find someone to share my bed with. There was a mutual understanding between me and the women I slept with. Sometimes things got dicey, but it wasn't anything I couldn't handle. Relationships were something I didn't want to deal with. Period.

Broderick looked behind him prior to turning back to me, a smirk firmly planted on his face. "Looks like Gage struck out."

His words made me turn around to confirm. Gage was now by himself, looking at his phone. "Bet he thought he was going to end up taking her downstairs." Broderick shrugged as I shook my head and downed the rest of my drink.

Another server walked by and said, "Can I get that for you, sir?"

"Yes," I said, and the man took the glass and placed it on his tray. I buttoned my suit jacket.

"Where are you going?"

"I have something I need to take care of. I'll probably be back." With that, I headed off to find out exactly what Anais was doing here.

It didn't take long for me to get down the stairs, but I had lost sight of them. Anais had somehow gotten into Elevate with what looked to be her roommate, based on the pictures and captions Dave had found on Anais's social media profiles. And I wanted to know how and why.

"Damien?" I glanced over and saw Kingston. He was my cousin and was doing us a favor by subbing in for one of Elevate's security guards who'd called out sick. He was stationed near the stairs to stop people who didn't belong in VIP from getting through. "Do you need anything?"

"No, I'm good," I said, just as I spotted the two women. They were making their way toward the bar. I walked around the periphery for a bit because I didn't want to draw attention to myself, nor did I want Anais to spot me before I was ready.

I watched as her roommate leaned over and whispered something in her ear and then she started making her way through the crowd leaving Anais alone at the bar. I knew it was my turn to strike. It took little effort for me to get to Anais and once I was close enough to touch her, I paused. She'd left her long brown hair down and it was a blessing and a curse because I thought about running my fingers through her hair while she gave me a blow job. The gold dress left very little to the imagination, and I could tell I wasn't the only one near her who thought the same. I noticed a guy to our right making his way over to her with his eyes stuck to her body as I assumed mine had been.

His eyes shyly shifted off of her and toward me and all it took was a look before he backed away. The person next to her grabbed their drink and shifted out of the way, leaving an opening for me.

I slid into the space and leaned down to ask, "What are you doing here?"

I could tell she was about to snap, but once her eyes landed on me, the words were gone. It took her a few seconds to recuperate from her shock but when she did, the feistiness returned.

"What do you mean what am I doing here? What are *you* doing here?"

"That's none of your business."

"And the reason I'm here is yours?" I saw a ghost of a smirk appear on her face, probably because she thought she'd won this battle. All I could think about was ripping that slinky dress off of her and fucking her on the bar. *In front of patrons? Why not?*

"Careful. You don't want to piss me off. And being that I'm the co-owner of this establishment and I don't like you being here because you're going to be mine, I could have you escorted out right now. Hell, I have no problem doing it myself."

I could tell when my words registered because her eyes widened. She knew I wasn't joking about doing it either.

"I haven't said yes to your arrangement. You're assuming that I will."

"I'm not assuming anything." I folded my arms across my chest. I was enjoying this sparring match a bit too much. The fire in her eyes was a stark contrast to the coolness that her green eyes had given off before. I knew she wasn't willing to go down without a fight and because of that there would be many good days and nights ahead. "You know what I'm looking forward to?"

"What's that?" I barely heard the words because she whispered them.

"Tomorrow, Spitfire." I turned around and took a step forward, back toward the VIP section.

But her words stopped me. "Don't call me that."

I turned back around and shifted my body closer to her. "I can call you whatever I want. Do you want to know why you'll come to me willingly?"

She was forced to look up at me even with the three-inch heels she was wearing.

"Because your father doesn't have the money and he won't have it by my deadline. You don't want to see Monroe Media Agency close. The stakes are too high." *In more ways than one.*

This type of deal wasn't something I usually did because I didn't have to. This time, I didn't want to take a chance that she would slip through my fingers. I wouldn't lie and say that I wasn't drawn to her when I first saw her photo. I let my gaze wander down her body before it made its way back up to her eyes. I could see that her eyes were staring at my lips when they drifted up to mine.

"But there's something else, Anais."

Before she could say anything, I bent my head down to kiss her, giving her a small preview of what it would be like to be mine. At first, she didn't react, but when she started to get into the kiss, I pulled away.

"You want to know what it's like to be fucked by me." I took a small step back and didn't fight my urge to smirk. "Wear something like this tomorrow." I turned and walked away, leaving her beautiful swollen lips ajar.

"Hey, Kingston," I said. "Have your men watch that woman in the gold while she's here tonight. She should be here with another woman. If she tries to make her way downstairs stop her." I had no problem monitoring her from my position in VIP.

"Got it. I'll switch positions and head toward that door just in case." Kingston leaned away from me and started talking into his earpiece, conveying the message I had just sent.

A smile crept onto my face as I walked back up the stairs to VIP. I knew that in a short period of time, Anais Monroe would be mine.

8

ANAIS

Coming here had been a bad idea. After Ellie told me about how she suspected Damien might own Elevate, I knew there was a chance that he would be here tonight. Now lo and behold, he was. My phone vibrated in my hand. I looked down and saw a text notification.

Damien: *Be ready at 7:30 p.m. tomorrow. My driver will pick you up.*

"You still haven't ordered a drink." Ellie appeared next to me.

"You almost gave me a heart attack. I forgot to order one."

"Is everything okay? We talked about it and then I went to the bathroom."

I leaned over to whisper in her ear, "I was preoccupied. Damien appeared."

"Wait, what?" Ellie's voice cracked, causing her to sound almost like a parrot.

If this were an everyday situation, I would have laughed. It wasn't and I couldn't bother to try to fake one.

"Yeah, and there's more that I need to tell you." It was time to come clean. I would do it once we got home.

"Okay. Do you want to stay here or head home now?"

I admired her for offering to go home with me even though we were in one of the most exclusive bars in New York City. Who knew when or if we would have the opportunity to do this again?

"No, let's stay. We should also at least get a drink while we're here."

"Good plan. This time I'll do the ordering."

I rolled my eyes at her little jab and turned to face the bar again. When we had our drinks in hand, I let the coolness of the mojito coat my throat in an attempt to calm down the raging fire that Damien's presence and words had caused to erupt. Ellie and I continued chatting among ourselves while drinking, but the entire time, I felt as if there was someone watching me.

"Did you want to go downstairs?"

"Downstairs? For what?" I played dumb even though I knew what she was referring to.

"To see what it's like? Supposedly, there is a lounge of some sort, or maybe it's another bar where people can meet other people and decide if they want to head farther into the club. I wouldn't want to go that far but figured the lounge might be a good place to get a feel for the atmosphere."

My mind drifted back to my interaction with Damien a few minutes ago before I came to a decision. I knew that if he found out what we were doing, it was going to further piss him off and I didn't care. I didn't answer to anyone and I could do whatever and whoever I wanted. Well that was what

I liked to tell myself, although I never had done anything like this before. "Sure, why not?"

I polished off my drink and followed Ellie as she made her way through the crowd. How she knew where the entrance to the sex club was, I would never know. We made it over to the bouncer, who I didn't remember seeing when I walked in, and Ellie turned on her charm.

"Hi, we would like to go downstairs."

"Are you both on the list?"

"Uh, maybe?"

I couldn't help but roll my eyes. She knew damn well we weren't on any list unless Ellie had done it without telling me.

"Where's your coin?"

She looked at me and then looked back at him. "What do you mean where's your coin?"

He looked at her and shook his head. "If you don't even know what I'm talking about, I know for sure that you're not on the list to get in. Please move aside."

"This is ridiculous. No one needs a coin to get in here."

"I said what I said. Now move aside." His stern voice told me he meant business and I noticed when his eyes stayed on her for a moment too long. Still, he didn't budge.

"Look—"

"Are you trying to start a fight with me?"

I grabbed Ellie's arm and she looked at me. "This isn't worth it, E. Especially if it's an invite-only type of thing."

"I think you should listen to your friend."

I could feel the anger in Ellie about to boil over. "You're being completely asinine about this because there is no coin needed for entry!"

"Big words there and you're annoying me."

"I don't care if I'm annoying you. Listen—"

"No, and now I'm going to escort both of you off the premises."

I could see Ellie fuming and if we were in a cartoon, smoke would have been coming out of her ears. The bouncer walked us halfway to the door when I paused for a second and looked up and saw Damien standing at the balcony. I didn't know how long he had been standing there, but the look he was giving me and the small wave he sent my way told me he had something to do with us getting kicked out of Elevate tonight.

∽

"That guy was such an asshole."

"Ellie."

"You don't need a coin to get into the club. I would have known."

I watched Ellie pace back and forth in front of me. Hopefully her stomps weren't loud enough to piss off the tenants underneath us.

"Ellie."

"He kept us out of there on purpose."

She definitely had that right, but she was giving me a headache on top of the thoughts that were already doing laps in my brain. "Ellie."

"I can't stand—"

"Ellie!" My hollering did the trick.

"What?" She stopped walking to look at me. "What's wrong?"

"There are some things I need to tell you."

She walked over and sat next to me on the couch and curled her feet up under her. That was when the dam of words broke. I walked her through everything that had fallen in my lap over the last few days. Monroe Media Agency's impending collapse, my father going to Damien Cross for money to help save the agency from failing, and then Damien approaching me about the deal.

"Oh, honey," Ellie said for what seemed like the fiftieth time. "I take back everything I said about you becoming involved with Damien. Fuck him, excuse the pun. We'll figure out a way to get you out of this."

If I wasn't worried about the situation, I would have laughed. "I feel like I have no choice but to say yes." I ran a hand across my forehead and into my hair. I barely stopped myself from yanking the strands.

"No, there has to be another way. We can go to the police."

"Ellie, we can't call the police. They probably wouldn't believe me anyway, and I don't want my father to know any of this."

"There has to be some way to get you out of this. Maybe if we both take out loans. I could try going to my parents..."

Ellie's words made my head snap in her direction. I stared her down for a moment before the words I wanted to use came to me. "There is no way I would drag you into this."

"Shit," she mumbled. She kept whatever else she was thinking to herself.

"I know."

Ellie closed her eyes for a moment and when she opened them, they zeroed in on me and it didn't take much for me to read the sadness in them. "At the very least, if you go through with it, it's only thirty days, right? If you could stay strong for thirty days, maybe it won't be so bad? None of this sits right with me."

Me either. I thought about Ellie telling me that he had enough money to make me disappear with the flick of his finger, but if he could do that to me, he could do it to my father as well.

Visions of that happening to my father crowded my brain and involuntarily made me shiver. I muttered a cuss word and threw my head back on the couch. I assumed it meant that anyone that was in my family or close friend circle would have a target on their backs if Damien didn't get either his money or me.

It was a few moments before I sat back up and gasped. "There's one thing I forgot to tell you!"

"Well?"

"The night I went to have dinner at my parents' house, some random man shoulder-checked me on the way back to our apartment. He told me to watch myself. I also thought I might have been being watched at Elevate but wrote it off as me being paranoid. After all, it was hard to not have at least someone's eyes on you when you're in a crowded place."

"Based on what we now know Damien is capable of, I wouldn't put it past him to have you being watched."

"Me neither. Plus, it would feed into his desire to intimidate me."

"When is the deadline for having to tell him?"

"Tomorrow. He told me to be ready by 7:30." I opened his message on my phone and showed it to Ellie. "It's not even worth me running away."

"Nope, because he'll find you. The only way I could see this working out is if you could get all of the money your father owes him by tomorrow, but we both know that's damn well impossible."

"Yeah, I know." I ran a hand through my hair and watched as my tresses fell onto my shoulder.

Ellie grabbed my other hand and squeezed. "Just remember, you need to make it out unscathed. You can't get addicted to him."

"That won't be hard. I hate the man."

～

THE NEXT EVENING, I watched as the time grew closer and closer to when I was supposed to be picked up. I could finally admit to myself that I would go to him, but I'd be damned if I was going to wear anything that resembled the dress that I had worn last night at Elevate. I threw my hair up into a high ponytail and changed into a green sweater, fresh denim jeans, and white Chucks that had seen better days. I looked more like a student than a working professional nine years removed from her college days, but I didn't care. I wasn't going there to please him; I was doing this to save Monroe Media Agency and all of its employees. And if he didn't want me this way, that wasn't my problem.

That pep talk helped energize me for whatever would happen tonight. That was the thing: I didn't know what was coming next, nor did I know what to expect and I was sure he'd use that to his advantage. When the clock struck 7:28 p.m., I stood up and zipped my winter coat. I double-checked that I had my mace with me and closed my purse. It was better to be safe than sorry.

I shuffled toward the front door, my heart pounding harder with every step.

I watched as a set of headlights appeared at the corner of my street. The car moved past my building and, as I stepped out, the driver made a U-turn before pulling in front of my building and parking the car. A man in dark-colored clothes stepped out of the vehicle and, based on what I could see, he was the man who had picked up Damien from the Project Adoption gala.

"Miss Monroe?" he asked, which was him being polite because I was pretty certain he already knew who I was if my assumptions about Damien were correct. He was wearing what looked to be a black suit, which matched the sedan's exterior. He looked more muscular than he had the night that Ellie and I saw him, but that could be my fault for not paying much attention to him because Damien had dropped his demands on me.

I rolled my shoulders back and looked him in the eye. I refused to be intimidated. "Yes, that's me."

"Right this way. My name is Rob and I'll be taking you to Mr. Cross's home this evening," he said as he opened the door.

I stepped inside, without saying another word and he closed the door behind me.

Something in me was expecting to see Damien sitting inside the car just to throw me off, but he wasn't there, so I had more time to myself before I had to deal with Satan in the expensive suit. Once Rob stepped into the driver's seat and closed the door behind him, I heard the locks engage and I wondered if he had done it on purpose to keep me prisoner or if that was an automatic feature of the car.

"Could you tell me where we're going?" I asked, just as Rob pulled out of the parking spot.

"We are going to Mr. Cross's home. Let me know if you need anything." He gave me a small smile and raised the divider between us.

I knew that was done as a way to get me to stop asking questions because he hadn't given me the answer I wanted. Soft jazz tunes played in the background as we glided through New York City's streets. Since I was alone, all I could do was think of all the different scenarios that might come about tonight. An idea popped into my head and I pulled out my cell phone to send my location to Ellie just in case something terrible happened. Once I had done that, I put my phone away. At the very least, someone would know where to start looking for my body. The thought of that made me tremble as I tried to ease concerns that something might happen to me.

The ride to Damien's gave me even more time to think about his deal. Taking this deal didn't mean that he got to set all the rules. There were some hard limits to what I was willing to do and he was going to hear about them tonight whether he liked it or not. Some of the items I wanted to discuss I had been mulling over, but several of them I thought of on the drive to Damien's. I typed them up on my phone to pass more time on my journey to what I called hell.

About twenty-five minutes later we were pulling up to a townhouse and I was somewhat shocked we were still in Manhattan. Rob carefully parallel parked the car as I held on to my phone like a crutch, hoping that it would calm my nerves because at least I had that lifeline still available to me.

"I'll walk you up to the front door." With that, he opened the door, letting himself out.

"Well, at least I won't be going on my death march by myself," I mumbled, making sure he didn't hear me.

Rob stepped out of the vehicle and I watched him walk around the car before he reached my door. Every step he took made the blood rushing through my ears louder. I looked around and found myself on a relatively quiet Manhattan street that was filled with other townhomes that looked just like the one I was standing in front of. I waited for Rob and together we walked up the stairs to the front door.

"How long have you been working for Damien?" I asked.

"I've worked for Mr. Cross for seven years now."

"Hmm. So I'm sure you've seen a lot."

He didn't respond, which told me all I needed to know. That did little to help my anxiety as we stood in front of the door.

"If you need anything, just press the number one on any phone in his place. I'm sure he'll tell you to do the same."

I nodded and he walked down the stairs as I was left staring at the red door. I knocked on the door and took a step back. I held my breath, awaiting what would be my fate.

9
DAMIEN

"And you need to be here at 10 a.m. in order to catch the meeting with Ben Nichols. Information for that meeting will be on your desk and in the calendar invite."

"That should work. Thanks, Melissa."

Melissa had been my assistant for about three years, and I admit I would be much more disorganized without her even if it meant her staying at work until after seven to make sure I had everything I needed.

"Is there anything else you needed?"

"That will be all."

"Have a good evening."

I hung up my phone and walked into the dining area. I watched as Lucy, my personal chef, finished lighting the candles on the dining room table and I checked my Rolex. Anais and Rob should be arriving in about five minutes. I knew Rob was always punctual so if they were late, it was more than likely a result of Anais being stubborn. It was something I was looking forward to yet was the exact opposite of what I usually went for when it came to finding someone to fuck.

"The apple pie should be done pretty soon, but you'll need to set it out to cool on the wire rack. I put that right there." Lucy pointed diagonally behind her. "I have everything else either covered up so that it stays warm or in the other oven."

I nodded and she walked around me before she headed toward the hallway that led to the front door.

"Good night, Mr. Cross."

"Night."

She closed the front door, and I was alone once more. Some might say a house with five bedrooms and six bathrooms was excessive for one man, but I didn't care about what other people thought I should do with my money. Plus, the only reason the public really cared was because the tabloids wrote about it and it sold copies. It was a never-ending cycle.

A glance around my home told me that everything was perfect. The cleaning service had finished up several hours ago, so my home was immaculate. Although I was barely here, it didn't hurt to have someone freshen up the house frequently. I'd bought this townhouse several years ago when I decided I wanted to have somewhere to lay my head down in NoHo. It didn't hurt that the house had a gym already in the basement. One less thing I needed to wait to have built. It also wasn't unheard of for me to stop by for a quick workout after a conference call and grab lunch here before the next event or meeting I needed to attend.

The wine room was heavily pushed by the seller's real estate agent as a bonus. I walked over to my bedroom door and locked it without looking inside. That was the last place I wanted her to go in case she had decided to snoop. Something told me if she got the chance, she would take it. No one stepped foot in there without my permission.

I couldn't deny that I enjoyed Anais's grit and determination to fight to get what she wanted even if it meant fighting me to get it. I was used to having people fall over me to make sure that I was well taken care of, and it was a nice change of pace to have someone who wouldn't just take my shit. It also made the fight and eventual takedown even better. I knew this experience would be enjoyable for both of us once she learned what being mine was all about. And she would learn quickly.

I walked back into the kitchen and looked at the notecard Lucy had laid out on the counter for me. She had done everything that I had requested to prepare for tonight's meal. Part of me wondered if I was doing too much as I saw the candles flickering out of the corner of my eye. Was I trying to get a good reaction from Anais by doing all of this? I would say so, but only so that I could catch her off guard and get my way in the end. To make her think that this little arrangement would be no big deal as I laid my requirements on the table. She didn't know what she was getting herself into and I looked forward to her reaction. I checked the clock again and straightened my suit jacket. I went for my standard all-black suit without a tie. I ran a hand through my hair and then there was a knock on the door.

"Right on time," I said to myself as I took one more sweep of the room before heading to the front door. So, she hadn't put up a fight to come here. *Interesting.*

I looked at myself in the hallway mirror that my interior designer had insisted on installing and made sure that I had gotten nothing on my suit. I opened the door and startled Anais based on her wide-eyed look.

"This isn't what I had in mind when I said you should wear something similar to the dress you had on at Elevate." An image of her in the shimmery gold dress that ran on repeat in my mind made my dick shift. I could have said hello first, but where was the fun in that? Plus, it was the truth. I expected her to be rebellious given the conversations we'd had, but I hadn't been expecting this.

"I must have forgotten," she said with a shrug as she entered my home. "I'm surprised you opened your own door."

"I'm very capable of opening a door. But you don't seem to be capable of following directions. That will be rectified." My words had their intended effect when she averted her gaze before facing me once more. I gestured for her to walk into the foyer and I closed the door. She looked back for a second before she walked farther down the hallway.

"I'm shocked your place is nice. Then again, you have enough money to buy anything, including women."

I knew she was doing her best to change the subject, but this wasn't the last she was going to hear about her ability to not listen to my instructions.

Is her plan today to cause as much irritation as possible? Nice try. "Thank you. Dinner should be ready in a few. I'll take your coat. We'll go downstairs and pick out a bottle of wine." She handed me her coat and I placed it in the coat closet.

"I didn't say I wanted a glass of wine."

I raised an eyebrow at her since I had done my homework. "Follow me."

I nodded my head and walked toward the stairs leading to

the basement. I flicked on the lights and walked down with Anais trailing behind me.

"Pick any bottle." I held open the glass door that led into the wine room.

It seemed as if Anais's mouth was permanently open as her gaze moved from bottle to bottle. "Some of these bottles of wine have to be hundreds of dollars."

"Some are even a few thousand."

It took a few seconds, but she closed her mouth and continued studying the bottles of wine. Finally, she picked one. "Here, I'd like to try this one."

"Excellent choice, this bottle is from Tuscany."

A ghost of a smile appeared on her lips briefly before it vanished. "Is this a thousand dollars?"

"It's not." I didn't tell her that it was damn close to it. "All right, come on and I'll open this up." I let her go upstairs first before I turned the lights off and followed.

Once we were upstairs, I walked past her giving her the opportunity to roam around the open area that was my living room, kitchen, and dining room. I poured myself a finger of whiskey into a glass I'd set out a few moments ago. While I was opening the wine bottle, I glanced up to find her examining my home.

"If it wasn't cold outside, I'd take you up to the roof so that you could see all of Manhattan."

"I wouldn't be interested."

"Don't lie to me."

I grabbed both glasses and walked over to her. She settled on looking out the window closest to my couch. When I approached, she took a seat on my couch and I handed her the wine glass. Small talk during regular business meetings annoyed me to no end and this wasn't much different. "So, you decided to come, which means you are agreeing to our deal."

"Yes, but I'm going to negotiate the terms." She leaned forward and placed her wine glass on the coffee table.

"You think you have negotiating power in this situation?" It was amusing to think that she did, and I could see that she was getting upset.

Her eyes darted around the room and she clenched and unclenched her hands. She was probably imagining slapping me across the face and the thought forced me to hide any excitement. I dared her to do it in my mind just so she could experience what type of punishments I would unleash if she defied me.

"So what you want me to do is strip and lie on my back, so that I'm in prime position for you to take me whenever you want? Is that what you want? Well here, then." She pulled off her sweater and I saw hints of the plain black bra she was wearing underneath.

I scoffed as I leaned forward to place my glass on the coffee table next to hers. "Stop. Is this your way of exerting power? You have no leverage here, Anais. It's cute that you are trying to act as if you do though." I could see when the realization hit her because her entire mood changed. Her face switched from being upset to downright angry. What she did next surprised even me.

She whipped out her cell phone and lay back on my couch. She ignored me for several seconds and I leaned over and snatched the phone.

"Hey—"

"Are you trying to order a vibrator?" I asked. There wasn't

much in this world that surprised me, but I would admit that this did it. My lips twitched as a chuckle threatened to come out my lips. "Is this supposed to get under my skin?"

"I figured since I wasn't going to get any pleasure from this, a vibrator would be an excellent investment. Or maybe I can grab mine from home."

"You won't be needing any kind of toy unless I'm the one using it on you. Here's the thing, Anais. You control nothing for the next thirty days. I do. I control your pleasure and everything else. When and how, it's all up to me. Once you understand that, this arrangement will be beneficial for both of us. Now we are going to sit down and enjoy a meal together."

I knew the edge in my voice got to her because her eyes refused to meet mine. My little speech had rendered her temporarily tongue-tied because all she could do was look down at her hands. The dinging of my oven timer cut through the tension.

"Dinner?" she asked, her head shooting up from its prior position.

"Yes, you know the meal that comes after lunch?" I asked her with an eyebrow raised. I stood up from the couch and made my way to the kitchen. My open-concept townhouse allowed me to easily see her in the living room from the kitchen. "That would be the pie that Lucy left."

Her eyes turned to me. "Who is Lucy?"

"My personal chef."

She visibly relaxed at my answer. *Fascinating.*

"Hiring a chef was the best option for me because of work and traveling." I put on an oven mitt and turned to grab the pie out of the oven.

"Or you could just meal prep like the rest of us."

I silently chuckled to myself before I said, "What was that?" I stood up and turned to face her, placing the hot dessert on the counter.

"Nothing. I said nothing."

This might be more fun than I thought after all.

10

ANAIS

Dinner was awkward to say the least. I stayed quiet, only opening my mouth to eat the meal that Damien's chef had left for us. The melt-in-your-mouth lobster tail was delicious, along with the truffle mac and cheese and sautéed spinach.

"There's pie for dessert."

I thought it was a bit much to make all of this food for someone who was coming over to settle a debt. Then again, it wasn't like Damien had spent the time making it himself. I didn't know how I was going to fit any more food in my stomach after what we'd just eaten. That, however, didn't stop me from nearly polishing off my second glass of wine. I hoped it would help calm the anxiety I was feeling about what would happen after dinner was over.

"More?" he asked, gesturing to my almost empty wine glass.

I shook my head because my goal was to keep a straight head and two glasses would keep me there.

As I took another sip of the wine, I looked around the

townhouse that Damien called home. I would describe it as a bachelor pad, although the outside of the house looked like a pretty standard New York City townhome. The modern-sleek dark décor that was in Elevate was present in his home, which made me wonder if Damien or his interior designer played a part in the club's design. The wood floors were stunning and something I hoped to have one day when I owned a home.

"What time can you move in tomorrow?"

I glared at Damien. "Say what?"

"You heard what I said."

"And I can't believe that you still have the ability to leave me flabbergasted. I'm not moving in with you. I refuse to pay rent for my apartment if I'm not living in it."

"You won't have to worry about that because it will be taken care of. The entire thing."

I raised an eyebrow. "You mean Ellie's portion too?"

"The entire thing. I don't like to repeat myself, Anais."

My mouth had no filter when it came to Damien. I also couldn't help myself, but something inside of me worried that I might dig a deeper hole and I still had so much to lose. He shouldn't be allowed to treat me or anyone else like this. I thought that my words might anger him. Instead, he gave me a small smile.

"You and I are going to have a lot of fun."

His voice deepened when the word *fun* fell from his lips, sending a small current of electricity through my body that I refused to acknowledge. There was still fear, however. Fear about not knowing what he had in mind or what he had planned. That seemed to be one tactic he used to keep his enemies guessing.

"You're moving in here and there's no room for discussion. If you don't, the deal is off and I don't think you can afford that, can you?" His words sent a tremble down my spine. Once again, he was right. I couldn't afford for the deal to be off. Too many people were counting on me to cancel this debt, even if they didn't know it.

"Can I make one request?" I asked, attempting to take a fresh approach.

He shrugged his shoulders. "You're allowed to ask. Doesn't mean I'm going to grant it."

I placed my fork down on the table and folded my hands. I peeked out the window before turning my attention back to Damien. "I don't want anyone to know that this is happening."

He tilted his head to the side, seemingly digesting my request. "Are you trying to keep me as your dirty little secret?"

I rolled my eyes. "Call it what you want. I don't want people to know that the reason why you and I are together is because I am trying to settle a debt on behalf of my father. That includes my parents. Now, I assume that there will be questions if we're ever seen out in public, but I want to keep this as tight-lipped as possible. I also want it down in writing that you will cancel this debt once the conditions are... met."

"I can work with that."

I was shocked I was able to get that minor victory, but I didn't make a big deal about it. "I also still need to go to work because Monroe Media Agency clients count on me to do my job." I had the ability to work from home and flexible leave, but that wasn't something I wanted him to know. "Oh, and I don't want to sleep in the same bed as you."

"Anais, you will get used to the idea of what I say goes. I

had no intention of you not going to work or doing your job so you're in the clear there. And you won't be sleeping in my bed because I don't sleep with anyone. I sleep alone."

I mentally thanked Ellie because his revelation didn't startle me. I watched as he placed his utensils on the table and a dark look took over his face. The smile that appeared didn't do him any favors either.

"I can't wait to break you." His voice was low and deep, causing the words to come out sinisterly.

"So that means I'll have my own room?"

He nodded. "You'll have your own room and bathroom. No one enters my bedroom but me unless I give you permission."

That was the first time I had felt relieved all night. At the very least, I would have my own space away from him. But it did draw up questions about why he was so protective of his bedroom.

"I assume since you have a chef that you have a cleaning service. Are they not allowed in there either?" I asked the question as innocently as possible, hoping to not make him suspicious about the fact that I was digging for information. I hadn't planned on entering his bedroom, but the secrecy made the red flags in my mind fly high and proud.

"They are, but they mind their business."

I had to force myself not to roll my eyes as I picked up the double meaning behind his words. "You make it sound as if you have a red room or something."

He snickered. "Funny you should mention that because we are going to go to Elevate at some point soon. That way you don't have to beg and plead for Kingston to let you into the basement."

"I did nothing of the sort." I could feel my body betraying me due to his comment, but I would never admit to it.

He sat back in his chair and folded his arms with a smug look on his face. "Yes, you and Ellie did, and I'm sure it was just to see what was going on down there. I'm happy to take you on a tour of the aspects of Elevate that you haven't seen yet. Trust me, there are plenty."

"Oh, no."

He can't do this.

"Oh, yes."

Yes, he can do this.

"I already told you, I'm in control of your pleasure and it will be a *pleasure* for me to take you there."

I could feel my pulse racing. I raised my hand and placed it on the side of my neck. *He can't be serious, can he?*

One glance at his face told me he was.

I cleared my throat and said, "Last, I want us to be monogamous during this arrangement."

"Is this in reference to my reputation?"

I did my best to keep my voice even. "No. This is something that I wanted and thought you might agree."

He didn't answer right away, and I couldn't tell if he was thinking about my suggestion or doing this on purpose to make me sweat. If I had to be honest with myself, it was a bit of both.

"That works for me since I don't share what's mine."

"I'm not yours."

"You are for a month."

He had me there.

Damien pushed back from the dining room table, stood,

and walked over to the living room area. "Why don't we get started now?" He tossed the question over his shoulder.

I thought the way I dressed to come to dinner would have turned him off. I jumped up and stomped behind him, my heart rate picking up speed. "But I'm not dressed—"

"Whose fault was that? You seem to have a very hard time following directions." He sat down on the couch and lazily let his eyes roam over my body. "Did you think that just because you dressed down that would stop me from collecting what's owed to me?"

The smug smile appeared once more on his face and I wanted to knock it off.

This was all a game to him. "Since you were in such a hurry to take off your sweater earlier, why don't you do it now?"

I didn't move right away. I disliked this man more than anyone I had ever met, yet his words started a small ember in my body that I couldn't control. Ellie's words about not getting addicted to him rang in my ears as I moved to take off my sweater.

"Wait a second," he said, pulling out his phone. A few swipes led to the blinds closing, and the lights in the room dimmed to a warm hue. "Stand up."

This time instead of giving him any attitude I did as I was told.

This is only for a limited time. You can make it through this, Anais.

"I said, take off your sweater."

I turned, took off my sweater, and let it fall to the ground with a soft thump. I stalled. It wasn't that I was ashamed of my body. I worked out pretty regularly and ate healthy most of the time and I knew it showed. But feeling his gaze burning a hole into my back stopped me from turning around because I would have to face his gaze head-on.

"Anais." His voice was stern with a hint of annoyance. That was what finally got me to turn around. "Was that so hard?"

Don't answer him. It will only encourage him to act more like an asshole. The ember that he lit under my skin continued to grow, although I did my best to tamp it down. His inspection of my body made the tension in the room thick as a cloud of billowing smoke and I could feel my nipples harden as they brushed up against the soft yet firm fabric of my bra. I couldn't even blame it on being cold because it was warm in his home.

"Take off the bra and touch yourself."

"What do you—"

I watched as Damien's eyes darkened. "I'm not repeating myself again."

My eyes migrated down from his eyes to his chest and cock. Although it was more difficult to see beneath his pants, I could tell that he was affected by the display he wanted me to put on. A slip of his tongue peeked out from his lips. I could feel my cheeks heating although I wished they wouldn't. This wasn't my first rodeo, although I had never been with someone who was this demanding.

My hands made their way toward my back and unhooked the bra. I let it fall off my shoulders and watched it hit the floor with a light tap. They then journeyed to my breasts, gently massaging them as I imagined he would do. But who was I kidding? I knew he would be rougher than that.

I got up enough nerve to look him in the eye and noticed

that his eyes veered from looking at my movements to looking back at my face, as if he were studying me. I wasn't expecting him to stand up so when he did, I took a step back and immediately scolded myself for doing so. He took another step toward me and I stood my ground and didn't move an inch. I didn't even try to breathe because I didn't want him to mistake that for me being intimidated.

"I'm looking forward to our time together." His tone took on a rough, raspy timbre that sent a jolt through my body. His eyes said something more, but I was having a hard time reading them. However, his words soon tossed clarity on the table, making it easy for me to understand. "Stop touching yourself and put your clothes on. Pack your things tonight and I'll see you tomorrow."

His words were like ice-cold water being dumped on my head and they snapped me out of my thoughts, making me realize that once again, this was all a part of the game he was trying to play with my mind and body. What sucked was that my body betrayed me and no matter how much I tried to deny it, I wished that it was his hands on me instead of my own.

Damien backed away from me and left the room without tossing another glance my way. I threw on the clothes as if my ass were on fire. I had been dismissed without a care in the world and I didn't know how to process it. When I made myself presentable, I rushed to the closet where Damien hung up my coat and didn't even have time to throw it on before I dashed out his front door. As I left the townhouse, I saw Rob sitting in the car. The slam of the front door behind me caused him to look over and a moment later he got out of the sedan. I walked away from the door, putting my winter coat on one arm at a time, and by the time I reached the car, Rob already had one of the back doors opened for me. Rob slightly nodded his head in acknowledgment but said nothing.

I wondered how often this happened. Ellie had mentioned that Damien had his fair share of women come and go, but had he made similar arrangements like this in the past? *Wait. Why did I care?* I shifted those thoughts in my head as the car started moving. Once I was settled in the car, I laid my head back on the chair and let the events of this evening replay in my brain. As I thought about it, anger rose in my veins replacing feelings of humiliation, embarrassment, and shock that I'd felt previously.

How dare he just kick me out like that? I wished I had gathered up enough courage to say something when he was in front of me, but I had been overwhelmed, given how quickly everything was happening. I needed to school myself on how to react to him and his mind games because I was sure this wouldn't be the last time this would happen.

What shook me to my core was realizing that I was fooling myself. I wasn't pissed because he had humiliated me before kicking me out. I was pissed because I liked it.

11

ANAIS

"Hello?" I called as I walked through the front door because I didn't know if Ellie was home.

She peeped her head from around the corner and that was when I noticed that water was running in the sink. "Hey! I was just washing dishes while I waited for you to come home. How did it go with Damien?" Her eyes widened and before I could say anything, she jetted back into the kitchen. The water shut off and she came flying out of the kitchen, wiping her hands on a dish towel.

"It went," I said, and I closed the door and walked into our apartment. I didn't even bother taking off my coat and then I flopped down to the couch. I put my hands over my face, and I tried to figure out what I was going to say. "So, he had his personal driver pick me up and he had dinner set out and ready to go when I got there."

Ellie sat down next to me on the couch. "That sounds sweet."

I looked at her in disbelief. "Sweet? That is the last thing I would use to describe Damien." My voice was muffled because of how hard I was pressing my hands against my face.

"Well, keep going," she said, clearly impatient and wanting to know the entire story.

"He told me to move in with him."

"Shut up." She paused to look at my reaction. "You're not kidding. What?"

"Yeah. For the next thirty days."

"Are you gonna do it?"

"I haven't decided yet but according to him, I'm moving in tomorrow."

"That's quick." Ellie folded her legs under her.

"Tell me about it. I would think that at most I would have to bring clothes because his apartment is fully furnished."

"Well, if you decide to move in with him, I at least know where you are."

I had forgotten I sent Ellie my location on the way to Damien's place. That had been some good thinking on my part.

"Maybe it won't be so bad?"

I slowly turned my head to Ellie, not believing what she just said. "Maybe not, but it's not something that I want to do. He's only moving me in because he wants me at his beck and call."

"That's true, but maybe there are some amenities you could take advantage of?"

"He has a personal chef."

Ellie's mouth opened wide before she closed it. "I don't even know why I'm shocked by this. He probably shits hundred-dollar bills."

I couldn't help but snicker. "Or maybe he wipes his ass with them. You truly have a way with words."

"It's a gift. Anyway, stop getting sidetracked. What else happened after he mentioned you moving in with him?"

"I told him I was worried about having to pay rent so that we could keep the place after I leave. Didn't know if that would be added to my debt as well."

"Oh yeah, that's right." I couldn't believe Ellie forgot that part, but I gave her a little leeway given what I had just spilled to her.

"And he said he would pay the rent, no problem. Including your portion."

Ellie grabbed my thigh. "Say what?"

I confirmed with a nod of my head.

"I'm not sure how I feel about that."

"You and me both."

Ellie started playing with the ends of her brown hair. "Heck yeah, I want my rent paid, but also feels like we might end up owing him something outside of what you're doing."

"I know," I agreed once more, trying to wrap my head around the whole situation. I debated whether or not I should tell her about how he had me on display. I didn't know what good that would do besides potentially embarrassing me even more.

"I'm going to head to bed soon. I have a lot to think about and I'm exhausted."

"Sounds good. I'll see you later."

I turned off the lights in the living room and turned off the television for the night while Ellie wrapped up cleaning things in the kitchen.

I walked over to our window to close the blinds and just

as I was about to pull one of the blinds down, something caught my attention from out of the corner of my eye. From the apartment building across the street, there seemed to be someone pointing something at our window. I could see slight movements and when I saw a flash, it all but confirmed it was a camera. I stopped moving for a split second before I acted as if nothing had happened.

I backed away from the window, without closing the blinds, and said, "Ellie?"

"What? I was just getting ready to—"

I put my finger up to my mouth, signaling for her to be quiet. "Can you hit the lights?" She did as I asked and walked over to me.

"What's going on?"

"I think someone is spying on us from across the street. If we back up enough and walk around the couch, we should be able to look from both sides of the window to see if I'm right."

"Okay," she said, and we both walked out of the range of what we thought could be seen into our apartment before reaching the window and slowly moving our heads to peek out of it.

Ellie gasped and then said, "I think you're right."

"Yeah, but by who?"

Ellie slowly closed the blinds, returning the apartment back to our private sanctuary. "It could be Damien. Making sure that you're doing what he told you to do."

"But he wants me to move in with him, so wouldn't having someone watch me right now defeat the purpose?"

"You haven't moved in with him yet," Ellie pointed out. "Could be his way of keeping you under his thumb until you do."

"That's a good point."

Ellie clapped her hands together and said, "Or what if this is his way of pushing you into his arms?"

I raised an eyebrow at her. "Do you think Damien has ever had to work to get a woman to fall into his arms?"

"Touché."

"Can we go to the police with this?"

Ellie returned the eyebrow and scoffed. "Are you kidding? With what evidence? Although we suspect this person is spying on us, he or she could just be taking a photo of New York City architecture instead."

I sighed and pulled my ponytail tighter. "If I'm going to move in with Damien for a month, I want you to remain safe."

"Don't worry about me. I'll be fine. You're about to enter the lion's den."

~

I'D BE LYING if I said I didn't toss and turn most of the night. My emotions were all over the place as I thought about what the next thirty days would hold. I didn't want to move into his home. I enjoyed having my own space, and more than that, I hated the thought of sharing a space with someone who wanted me to move in so I could be his sex toy for a month. So, I did what any reasonable person would have done and sent a text to Damien.

Me: *This moving-in arrangement doesn't work for me. I have no problem meeting up with you somewhere, but I'm not moving into your home.*

There was a moment of relief that came when I hit send.

Panic soon replaced it as I realized I sent that message at three in the morning. I wasn't too keen on him knowing that I was up this late thinking about him. Part of me didn't care that I might have woken him up. but I valued sleep and felt a tinge guilty about disturbing someone else's. Or so I thought until my phone buzzed in my hand. I flipped my phone back over, thanking whoever created the ability to dim the light on your screen, and read the notification.

Damien: *You'll be moving in tomorrow. Rob will be at your place at 9 a.m. sharp.*

I almost screamed in frustration. The fact that Ellie's bedroom wasn't too far away was the only thing that stopped me.

Me: *I'm not ready and I don't want to go.*

Damien: *I'll come over there and carry you out myself.*

"Good luck with that," I said. Since it was 3 a.m. and there was no way I could pull myself together for anything tomorrow, I emailed my father and Vicki, his vice president, letting them know I was taking the day off. I tossed my phone to the side and looked at my room. I was in no shape to move anytime soon. Clothes were everywhere because of me being too busy between work and life. Shoes weren't in their proper place in my closet. I made a note to myself to spend part of tomorrow cleaning for my own well-being because I had no plans to go to Damien's. I got up and closed the curtains. I flopped back onto my bed and turned over.

I fluffed up my pillow and placed it back under my head, wishing that sleep would overtake me. It wasn't too long before it did, but there were no dreams to be had tonight. Only darkness as I pondered what tomorrow would bring.

~

ALTHOUGH I HAD GONE to bed super late, I still woke up early because my body was used to getting up early for work. I was super sluggish seeing as how I was operating on about four-and-a-half hours of sleep. Nothing could be done about that besides drinking a ton of coffee. A quick glance at my phone told me it was eight in the morning and I had heard nothing from Damien after the conversation we had the night before. Shrugging my shoulders, I stood up and got my day started by grabbing that cup of coffee. Once that achievement was unlocked, I checked and saw that Ellie had gone to work. I started sorting through my clothes that were laid out around my room. I was done with that in about thirty minutes so next up was a shower. I stood under the hot spray feeling it beat down over my body as it helped to relieve some of the stress I had been feeling. Once I was dried off, I put my wet hair into a French braid and threw on a tank top and running shorts. I glanced at my phone again.

8:55 a.m.

Five minutes before I was supposed to go downstairs with whatever I wanted to bring to Damien's place. I placed my phone in my back pocket and walked into the kitchen as I thought of another chore I could do. Who knew avoiding moving in with someone could motivate you to clean up your apartment? As I was about to lean down to unload the dishwasher, there was a knock on my door.

After a quick debate with myself, I decided not to answer it. But when the person knocked louder, I hurried over to the door, not wanting them to bother the other tenants.

"What the hell? Clearly someone is either not home or

pretending not to be. Go away," I muttered. What if it was the person that we suspected of taking photos of us last night? I peeked through the peephole. The man that haunted my dreams and had become my worst nightmare was standing on the other side.

How could I forget that he had threatened to come over again himself and pick me up and carry me out of here? Denial swung and hit me like a brick. My fight-or-flight instinct kicked in and my immediate thought was to head toward the fire escape. As I moved to grab my running sneakers, his fist pounded on the door again, even louder this time.

"Anais, I know you're in there," his voice boomed, sounding as loud as someone who had a megaphone up to their mouth.

Even if I tried to make a run for the fire escape, there'd be a very good chance that Rob was waiting at the bottom. Without thinking twice about it, I walked back over to my front door and opened it.

He immediately stormed in causing me to back up unintentionally. The door slammed shut behind him and I was convinced that one of my neighbors would soon call the cops.

"Do you get off on defying me?"

I didn't respond, instead choosing to focus on the look in his eyes and the tone of his voice. His eyes darkened and he was definitely on edge.

"Anais, I asked you a question."

"No. I'm just not the type of person who jumps when you say to." I knew my mouth was going to get me in trouble.

"Looks like your lessons need to begin now."

Puzzled, I watched as he looked to his left, checking to see if we were alone. He grabbed my arm and pulled me over to my sofa and sat down.

"What are you—"

He lazily dragged a finger up and down my leg, causing goosebumps along the way. He took my phone out of my pocket and tossed it on the coffee table. "Lie down on my lap."

"Excuse me I'm—"

He stopped my words with a stare. His chest was rapidly moving up and down and I couldn't tell if it was due to all of the yelling and knocking that he had just done or if it was because he was aroused. There was only so far that I could push my luck and with that thought in mind, I laid down over his lap.

"What are you going to do? Spank me?"

The taunt had the opposite effect I wanted it to have.

"Funny you should mention it," he said, now running a finger softly up and down my spine. "And these little shorts you have on give me ample opportunity to do whatever I want."

His touch brought another shiver to my body. I hated myself for enjoying what he was doing to me as his finger made its way back down to my ass. He brushed a hand against my bottom before he smacked it.

A rush of air left my lungs, and I could hear the slap vibrating through my body. *He freaking did it.*

And then he did it again. The hits weren't hard enough to make me cry, but firm enough to make my pussy tingle.

And again.

I didn't trust myself to speak. I knew my words would betray me.

"No words, Anais?"

I still didn't respond.

"Such a shame. After all, I'm enjoying you in this position."

Another slap met my flesh. There was no way that my ass wasn't turning pink by now.

"I think we've reached an understanding now, don't you?" His words flew across me like a weighted blanket as his hands started a war on my body. They massaged the places he'd hit as they made their way to my center. Damien shifted my shorts and my underwear to the side letting a small breeze tickle my pussy. He slid two fingers inside of me and chuckled at what he found.

"You're soaking wet. I think you enjoyed that quite a bit. And I'd bet you enjoyed the show you put on for me yesterday too."

Before I could even think to speak, his hand started moving faster. A moan fell from my lips, the first sound I'd made in minutes. My breathing came out in pants as I tried to control my body's reaction to his motions, but it was useless. My body hadn't orgasmed in months and it was primed and ready for one right now.

"Are you close?" he asked.

All I could do was nod my head as I buried my face into his thigh. The sensations were so intense that it took all of my control to not roll off of his lap.

"I could stop right here and end it all."

When he stopped moving his fingers, I screamed, "No! Please don't stop."

He let out a noncommittal grunt and slapped my ass again before sticking his fingers back inside me. It was almost as if he hadn't stopped and I was ready and revving to go once more.

And it was then that he laid one last strike on my ass that sent me soaring and it was only because of my face being stuck in his lap that my scream was muffled this time. I hadn't expected to feel the rush of emotions that came about as a result of him playing with me on my living room couch.

"I'm in control of all of this. Next time you go against my orders, there'll be plenty more slaps and you'll count each one out loud. Now let's go."

There was no way both of us were going to make it out of these next twenty-nine days intact.

12

ANAIS

It took a few moments for me to pull myself together after Damien let me up. I headed into my bedroom to put on a pair of jeans and a T-shirt. Then I threw some clothing in my bag. I figured an overnight duffle would be enough for now. I could return to my apartment in a few days to get more things. I also grabbed my work bag, thankful that I hadn't bothered to take anything out of that and threw it over my shoulder. Just as I was walking out of my bedroom, Damien hung up the phone.

"Glad to see you're finally listening to directions. Better late than never. Let's go."

I bit my tongue as he walked to my front door and opened it. I snatched my phone off the coffee table and followed in his footsteps. Once I had locked up, I followed Damien down to the car where Rob was patiently waiting.

Rob helped load my things and opened the door to let me in. I quickly scrambled into the car, making enough room for Damien to fall in behind me, and raised an eyebrow at him when he didn't.

"I have another meeting that I need to attend not too far from here. Rob is going to take you to my place so you can get settled. I'll check on you after the meeting is over." Part of me wondered what kind of meeting he could have on this side of town. I didn't ask, scared to think that it might be something I didn't want to know. I saw his face as he left me in this car. Between the furrowed brow and the darkening of his blue gaze, I worried for the safety of anyone who was on the other end of the conversation with him. I nodded my head, and Damien took a step back, allowing Rob to close the door. When Rob pulled off, I strained my neck a little to look behind me, to see where Damien was. He had already started walking down the street, like a man on mission.

~

IT DIDN'T TAKE LONG to get us back to Damien's. Rob opened the door for me and offered to grab my bags, which I accepted. Once we were inside, Rob turned to me and said, "Here's the key to the front door and my business card. I'll take your things up to your room."

Rob brought my bags through the foyer and down a hall where I was able to get glimpses of Damien's home. From what I could piece together, his home was impersonal. There were no family pictures or books that I could see. It almost seemed as if he just came here to eat and sleep before hopping back up to conquer the next company.

The enormous TV I saw hanging on the wall when I glanced into the living room looked to have all the bells and whistles and screamed bachelor pad. I followed Rob until he stopped at an elevator and I gasped. Of course, Damien would have an elevator in his home.

When we entered, Rob pressed the number four, and the elevator took us to that floor. Neither one of us said a word. When we stepped off the elevator, Rob showed me to my room and placed my bags inside and then went back to stand in the hallway.

"You are not to go to the top floor at any point. Let me know if you need anything." And with that, he was off.

His warning followed him out of my room and when the door clicked shut, silence crept in, creating an unsettling feeling. The bedroom I was staying in looked like a dream come true with its wooden floors, floor-to-ceiling windows, and a king-size bed that required me to climb into it. It resembled a hotel room and that I was okay with. If my ten-year-old self could see this bedroom, I knew she would describe it as a bright neutral-colored room that reminded her of a princess room without the frills. The room was decorated in whites, grays, blush, and other neutrals. The room had a few abstract paintings in those colors hanging on the wall and the bed was piled high with pillows. I loved the ivory roses that were sitting on one of the end tables. Who wouldn't want to stay here if the circumstances were different?

I turned to the dresser and found several pieces of paper and a pen. I took my time reading through the document and saw that it was two copies of a contract dictating that Damien would wipe my father's debt clean if the conditions of our arrangement were met. His signature was on the last page. *He had kept his word.* Feeling wary about signing a contract that a lawyer hadn't looked over, I did it anyway and placed it back on the dresser.

I began unpacking and neatly placed my things in one of the dresser drawers. After that, I took a step back before pivoting to head to what I thought would be a closet. When I opened the door, I gasped in both surprise and horror.

The closet was filled to the brim with women's clothes. Clothes in all different colors and styles, including dresses, slacks, jeans, and T-shirts. It was much more than I could have ever dreamed. I could only imagine how much these things were worth. I pulled out a red dress and checked the tag. I was shocked that he got my size right, and then I was shocked it was Valentino, which I knew could retail for several thousand dollars. Had he bought these specifically for me or were these hand-me-downs from another mistress?

I picked up a white cashmere sweater and felt the material between my fingertips. This was without a doubt the real thing given how soft the fabric felt and I knew this sweater alone had to cost a couple hundred dollars. What was the point in buying me these clothes? To make sure that I fit neatly into his world? Although I enjoyed having new clothes like the next person, irritation rose in my body, because I didn't know what the purpose of all of this was. Thoughts of whether or not I should switch rooms crossed my mind because it would irritate him, but I decided it wasn't worth the hassle. Plus, I loved the room that I was staying in so that solidified my decision to stay.

I grabbed my phone from my back pocket, snapped a picture, and sent it to Ellie. After debating the idea in my head for a moment, I waited to talk to Damien about all this in person the next time I saw him. I tossed my phone onto the bed and continued unpacking, but it didn't take me long to get settled, since I didn't bring much. As evidenced by the wall-to-wall clothes in the closet, I didn't need the little I had brought.

Once I left the bedroom, I debated going downstairs to the living room or going upstairs to his bedroom and looking around. Curiosity got the best of me and I listened for any sounds. I softly strolled over to the stairs. Hearing no one, I walked up the stairs when I reached the top level, my eyes ventured off to look at the only door that was closed. Something told me that that was the master bedroom. I approached the door and tried the doorknob, but it didn't budge.

I rolled my eyes. I should have known he would have locked the door, given that he was forcing me to move in here and he knew I would be alone in the house at some point. Part of me wanted to pick the lock, but I didn't want a charge of breaking and entering on top of whatever punishment he would dole out. His punishment was meant to "correct" my behavior, but the opposite happened. The spanking made me feel more alive and aroused, something that I wouldn't have guessed in a million years. It was the quickest I had ever found my release, wonderful in theory, but I hated the idea that I wanted to do it again.

I turned around and headed back down the stairs. As I reached the landing, I heard the front door open. I nearly jumped out of my skin at how close I'd been to having to explain myself to Damien.

I put a hand on my heart as I tried to slow my breathing down and walked over to the stairs to meet Damien. Once I reached the next floor, the man of the hour looked at me with a raised brow.

"What are you doing?" His voice was thick with suspicion.

"I was walking back from my room. Last I knew, I could do that without having to run it by you." Technically, what I said wasn't accurate, but he didn't need to know that.

He shrugged, accepting my answer. "You should have everything you need. I'll take you on a tour of the rest of the house and if you need anything, Rob is the person who you should call."

"Okay."

He nodded and checked his watch and looked back at me. There was something brewing behind those crystal blue eyes, but I knew he wouldn't tell me. "Lunch should be delivered in about an hour."

"Sounds good."

Damien started to leave but stopped as he reached the door. He turned to look at me over his shoulder. "Anais, if you ever try to open my bedroom door without permission again, you won't like the consequences."

With that, he left me standing there speechless, wondering how he knew I had ventured to the top floor.

∼

DAMIEN HAD to take a call from work, so I ate lunch alone. I was glad. It gave me some breathing room, something I so desperately needed after having to shift my entire life to fit his. It was quite lonely, and I had only been here for less than a day. I usually took lunch meetings or would get lunch with a coworker so not having anyone around was strange. I looked around some more, purposefully avoiding his bedroom because there was no way I was getting in there anyway with him being home.

The sights I saw earlier barely scratched the surface of everything there was to do in Damien's home. I found out that he had a chef's kitchen, a gym, and what I'm sure might become my favorite room in the house, the wine room. Although the house looked compact on the outside, due to it being a townhouse, it had more amenities than anyone could ever want on its five floors, and that didn't include the terrace on the roof. Plus, it was in a prime location in NoHo. I could see why he wanted this place.

I daydreamed about what it would be like living here full time before shaking my head. There was no way that I could live with Damien. Now, if he moved and decided to leave me the house that would be a different story. How I wasn't about to crash from pure exhaustion right now was beyond me, but I knew I was running on pure adrenaline. I decided to go work out in his home gym.

When I got back to my room, I realized that although I'd worn my running sneakers over, I hadn't brought any workout clothes. I walked over to the giant closet that was filled to the brim with clothes. I searched around and found something appropriate to work out in and threw on a black sports bra and black workout leggings. The clothes fit well, almost like a second skin, and the fabric was breathable.

"How did he know my size?" I asked the empty room, not expecting an answer. The thought troubled me, but there wasn't much I could do about it at the moment.

I checked that my French braid still looked decent and grabbed my phone before walking toward the stairs.

I walked downstairs to the gym. There were quite a few machines including an elliptical, an exercise bike, and a treadmill, which was what I was hoping for. I also found some water bottles, some towels, and an extremely fancy water dispenser. I did a mental high five because I didn't need to go back upstairs to the kitchen to retrieve the water I had forgotten.

It didn't take me long to grab some water and to get set up on the treadmill. Once I had a podcast queued up and I finished my workout warm-up, I was ready to go. I was in the zone as I ran and listened to the words of social media leaders talk about the latest trends. It provided a great way to ignore that I was jogging in place versus actually being out and about on hilly terrains and smooth walkways.

Exercise was great for my brain and allowed me to feel as if the fog that was around me was clearing up. Once I finished my cardio, I hopped off the treadmill and wiped it down. I grabbed my towel and wiped the sweat from my body. Then I started doing my abdominal exercises on the floor in one corner of the room. I closed my eyes as I let the movements take over and tried to breathe deeply while I was performing each move.

"This isn't how I expected to see you, on your back."

Damien's voice was louder than the podcast episode and I jumped, interrupting the groove that I had going.

"Don't stop on my account."

"I was just wrapping up anyway. You can leave now."

By my tone, anyone else would have backed away, but Damien took several steps closer. He was in my personal space and acted as if it were his own.

"Don't you have something to do outside of bothering me?"

"I'm not bothering you because I own you. I tell you what to do, remember? Or do I need to remind you?"

I huffed. "What do you want?"

"I was looking for you because I wanted to. Your sessions start now."

"Nope. You don't get to order me around whenever you please."

He reached out with his hand and gently grazed my cheek. "That's exactly what I get to do." He dropped his hand as if my cheek burned him. "You have exactly twenty minutes to shower and when you are done, you are to be naked, face-down, ass up on your bed."

"And if I'm not?"

"Don't test me. You won't like the consequences, Spitfire."

13

ANAIS

I stood in front of the mirror looking at myself. If I had any sense of self-preservation, I should be walking into my bedroom and presenting myself to Damien. In part, the thought of that made me sick. What made me want to shake myself was that being with Damien made me...excited, and I hated him and my body for it. The thought of him putting his fingers inside of me again made me wet, but I'd never admit that to him. I tightened the robe that I threw on after my shower and heard my bedroom door open.

I knew I was in trouble.

"You refuse to do as I say at all costs, don't you?" He was leaning on the door frame of the bathroom and I stared at him through the mirror. "Let's see if you understand this. Go stand near the bed."

I turned around and he moved out of the way, barely giving me enough room to get by him. When my body brushed up against his, my desire for him grew, even though I couldn't stand him. This time I did what he asked, and I stood near the foot of the bed.

"Spitfire, now was that so hard?"

"Oh, go fuck yourself."

"No. I'm going to fuck you. Do you know how long I've waited for this moment? I've been very patient with your smart mouth, but maybe now it's time I fuck it."

He looked at me, studying me like he was a predator, and I was his prey. I knew I was about to meet my end. He was still dressed in his suit and put his hand on his bulge, feeling himself through his pants. I wasn't sure if I'd ever seen anything more mesmerizing.

My heart rate quickened, and my breathing became more and more heavy to the point where I wondered if I was going to hyperventilate from watching him touch himself. He hadn't whipped his cock out yet but based on the bulge that had formed in his pants I knew he was hard. He took measured steps toward me and when he was finally standing just inches away, he placed his index finger under my chin and lifted my head up so that I looked at him. My eyes were drawn to his lips and lingered a bit before they made their way up to his eyes. I gasped when I realized that this man had given me an orgasm, yet our lips had only touched once.

Until now.

I had never been one to get hot and bothered over kissing.

Until now.

When his lips landed on mine, my mind lost all thoughts of anything except Damien. My primary goal was now making sure that Damien Cross, one of the most powerful men in New York City, lost control.

The kiss became harder and he captured my lips between his teeth, tugging on my lower lip before consuming me once more. It caused my temperature to spike and sent my pulse racing as we both tried to get as close as we physically could to one another. With his body on mine, his hard body against my softer one, I was eager to rip his clothes off. That thought jolted me since I couldn't stand Damien, but I chalked it up to not having sex in months. A few seconds later, he slipped his tongue between my lips and groaned in response as our tongues declared war with one another, neither one of us wanting to be the winner for fear that it might stop. The sweltering heat that this kiss brought to my body was enough to send me off and we hadn't done anything else. Yet.

He broke the kiss first as he moved down toward my neck, where it was only a matter of time before he—

I moaned when he found the sensitive spot on my neck and continued to assault it, causing me to squirm and groan. All he did was chuckle and continue his actions. I was disappointed when he stopped and pulled back.

"Lie down on your back."

"I thought you wanted me with my ass up in the air?"

"The time for that has passed."

I did as he said, and he yanked open the top of my robe exposing my breasts. He wasted no time in going after what he wanted. He immediately placed one nipple in his mouth while his fingers massaged and played with my other nipple until it became a taut peak. He then switched breasts and I clenched the bed sheets. One of his hands made its way down my body and it wasn't until I felt his finger in my pussy that I almost jackknifed off the bed.

He let my nipple fall out of his mouth with a decisive pop and asked, "What do we have here?"

"Damien." His name came out as more of a moan.

"I thought you said you hate me. That doesn't sound like you hate me."

"I do."

"Your body doesn't," he said as he removed his fingers from me and took his time licking each and every one.

His actions made me almost want to scream at him and beg him to put his fingers back where they belonged.

It was as if we were communicating telepathically because he placed his fingers back between my thighs and I made a noise that I couldn't even describe. His fingers moved like a maestro, in very distinct motions, as if he were playing my body like an instrument. This time, he moved faster and when I felt a familiar tingle, he slowed down and gave me a dark smile.

"Tease."

He didn't deny it.

But what I thought was teasing turned into a whole new realm of pleasure when he added another finger to my heat, and it was quite literally all downhill from there. My legs involuntarily opened wider and when I realized it gave him the ability to increase his speed, I threw my head back in ecstasy.

"I'm getting close."

"Don't."

I balked at his words. He had to be joking.

"I can't hold—"

"I said don't." The deepness of his voice sent another wave of pleasure through me, making it even harder to control.

"Dam—"

"I'll tell you when."

The urge to let myself go as a result of his finger fucking

was becoming way too much to bear. If he didn't let me—

"Let go."

There were no words I could use to describe the feeling that was coursing through my body or the cry that fell from my lips when he finally let me over the edge. I felt him leave my body, but I was too exhausted to even look up to see where he went. That was until I heard his belt buckle. I looked back at him and he'd already removed his shirt. It took everything in me to keep my eyes on his face. His lean yet muscular body wasn't a shock to me. I felt the power under his hand and his slacks did little to hide his muscular thighs. I was shocked to find he had just taken the belt off and had thrown it next to me on the bed. Was he thinking about spanking me? Or tying me up?

He took off his pants and boxer briefs next, and I was mesmerized once more by his cock. His dick stunned me, and my eyes widened before I could control my expression. It was long, thick, and hard and I couldn't deny that I became wetter at the sight of it. He slowly walked forward again but instead of approaching me, he went to one of the nightstands in the room and opened the drawer. He took out condoms and tossed them on the bed next to the belt. He joined me on the bed and climbed over my body. He completely unwrapped my robe and leaned forward to kiss me on the lips again hard before he pulled away.

"Now I want that ass up."

I did as he asked without questioning and by the time that I was ass up, he was already lining up his cock at my entrance and diving in. His decision to fill me up completely in one go took me by surprise as the yelp that left my lips turned into a moan.

"I knew this pussy would be tight around my cock."

His words turned me on even more and when he slid out a little, I braced myself for him to launch himself back into me and when he did, I saw stars. His movements picked up velocity and at first, I could barely keep up, but once I started meeting his every pump he groaned.

I could feel myself getting close to the brink again, but there wasn't any way I was going to have a second orgasm. It was too much, and I couldn't do it again. "I can't."

"Yes, you can."

"No. I can't."

"I know you can." He slowed down a bit and began playing with my other lips and I groaned from the sensations.

When he stopped and started pounding into me again, that was all it took for me to go over the edge. "Damien, I'm—"

My words were cut off after I let out another unhuman-like sound and it wasn't long before Damien was following behind me. He slowed down to almost a dead stop as he leaned over me, putting his head on top of my sweaty back. When he pulled himself back up and slipped out of me, I collapsed onto the bed. I heard some rustling behind me, but I was too weak to move. I closed my eyes for what I thought was a minute.

Damien's voice made me open my eyes. His expression was emotionless as he zipped his pants and said, "Dinner will be at six thirty. Meet me in the dining room and don't be late. I suggest you clean yourself up first."

He turned and walked out, pulling the door closed behind him. As the door clicked shut, I felt used and lonelier than ever.

14

DAMIEN

"Shit!" My voice came out as a harsh whisper as my eyes sprung open. I glanced around the room, confirming that I was at home and in my bed. I wiped the sweat from my forehead and felt a headache forming. I had another nightmare tonight.

I got out of bed and threw on some pajama pants that I had haphazardly thrown on a chair in my bedroom. I left my room, closing the door softly behind me, and walked downstairs, thinking that that was the quietest way to head down to the main level. I went to the liquor cabinet and poured a finger of whiskey before sitting in a chair near my fireplace.

I watched as the embers in the fireplace flickered to the point of extinction. It seemed like a good idea to light a fire on a cool December evening, but what it ended up doing was making my mind drift to places it went only when I was asleep. Images of flames clouded my mind, and I couldn't shake them. I took another sip of the whiskey I poured for myself. I knew it wasn't wise because of the headache I was dealing with, but right now it didn't matter. I knew it was the wee hours of the morning, yet all I could do was stare at the light as it slowly dimmed. Nights like this weren't uncommon and lack of sleep was what my brothers would say was the reason I don't do relationships, but it was more than that.

I'd seen life given and taken away in a single instance, which would haunt me until the day I left this Earth, and there was nothing I could do about it. I finished what was left in my glass and stood up, ready to face the demons that came only when I closed my eyes. When the last ember went out, it was showtime for another party that occurred only in my subconscious.

Every time Mom asked me when I was going to settle down and get married, I shifted gears, refusing to answer. But I didn't want to bring anyone permanently into my personal hell. It's why having very casual relationships worked best. No harm, no foul. That was what made everything with Anais so much better.

Dinner with her tonight was less eventful because she was more quiet than usual, but I chalked it up to her being tired from her move here. The deal we struck, though, was one of pure magic. She'd stay here for thirty days, which should be plenty of time for the urge to fuck her to burn out, and by day thirty, it would be done. Yet now I was jumping through hoops to make sure that everything was perfect for her when she came over for dinner and inviting her to live with me. The demons that haunted my nightmares must have done a real number on me to even consider something like this.

But I had never made this type of deal with another woman. Nor had I had another woman move into my house for any length of time. Doing things spontaneously was not wired into my psyche and I admitted that this whole arrangement with her was an impulsive decision. When I hopped into anything in life, whether it was for work or in my personal life, I researched as much as possible before forming an opinion or making a decision. Here, I had done the complete opposite because I was drawn to her in a way I couldn't explain. I had to do whatever I could to make her mine, even if that meant spinning up this foolish deal.

Having a taste of her drew more attention to how this deal shouldn't be occurring and how clouded my judgment was. I knew it wouldn't happen again, for both her sake and mine. I shook my head at the idea. That was the whole point of her being here, or at least that was what I told myself.

I could let her go, that way I could guarantee that she would remain unscathed, but the selfish part of me refused. I knew I would always be the tattered man who seemed to have it all on the outside, but inside, I was miserable, and I knew she would get hurt from this deal.

They say that money can't buy you happiness, but in my case, it's money that can't buy you peace.

15

ANAIS

Several days later, I exited the elevator and looked around the corner to see if anyone was standing near my office door. Seeing no one, I walked as quickly as my legs would allow me to my office and took off my coat. I hung it on the back of my door and winced when I stretched a bit too far to place it on the hook. My eyes drifted toward my desk chair and I sighed. I gave myself a small pep talk and headed over to my chair.

Things had been weird since Damien had blown any expectations that I had in the bedroom out of the water. He hadn't come to fuck me since the first time. In fact, I barely saw him and only in passing. Conflicting feelings floated around my mind about it. I felt relieved to not have to feel his intimidation around every corner, but I secretly hoped we would go for another round...or two. As much as I wanted to tell myself I hated the situation I was in, he was right. I would come to him willing and wanting.

"Anais?" I looked up from my laptop and found my father standing at the door. "Do you have a minute?"

"Sure. What's up?"

Although he had asked a question, it felt as if he were making a demand. He didn't look angry, but I could tell he was taking a more measured approach with his words instead of speaking freely. Dad closed the door and sat down in one of the extra chairs in my office. He didn't speak right away and seemed almost hesitant to tell me why he wanted to talk. I sucked in a deep breath, waiting for what I was worried would be more bad news.

"You know I don't try to get into your personal business, but is there something going on between you and Damien Cross?"

It took every ounce of control that I had in my body to not react to his words. "What?"

"Are you two dating?"

"No." *Technically that wasn't wrong.* I had done my best to keep our arrangement under wraps and the only person I had talked to about this was Ellie, who I knew wouldn't tell a soul. She was my best friend and I trusted her, but she also knew how high the stakes were. "What gave you that idea?"

"This." Dad pulled out his phone, swiped a few times, and then handed it to me.

There was Damien and me all right. The picture was blurry and grainy, but I knew it was from the night that Ellie asked me to go to Elevate with her. The gold dress that I was wearing was unmistakable and we were standing in front of the bar on the main floor of the club. I was relieved that the photographer hadn't caught the explosive kiss we'd shared. Looking at the photo, it would be hard to tell who either person was, especially Damien, whose back was to the camera. I moved my thumb along my father's phone screen, hoping to discreetly check who might have sent the photo. The email in the field was a nonsensical address filled with random letters and numbers, but the subject contained my name. Who was the person who snapped the photo and then leaked it? Wasn't Elevate supposed to have tight security against this type of thing?

My focus turned to the man who shoulder-checked me and the guy Ellie and I believed was spying on us near our apartment. Someone was tracking me. I turned away from my father to hide my trembling lip. I closed my eyes and took a deep breath, trying to calm the fear that was running through my veins. There was no way these incidents were all a big coincidence.

Damien. He always seemed to be several steps ahead of me and nothing seemed to happen without his approval, so he had to know about this. The anger built up inside of me, but I did my best to keep it under control in front of my father. Although I was an adult and could do what I wanted when I wanted, the last thing I wanted him to do was to get a whiff of this and tie it back to the debt.

"Ellie and I ended up at a nightclub the other night and Damien was walking around asking people if they were having a good time. Maybe he owns the place? Anyway, I told him I was and that was it." I knew I didn't have to explain myself to anyone, but if it stopped any suspicion, it needed to be done.

Dad's eyes shot down to the photo before looking back up at me. My anger turned to guilt. I hated having to tell even the smallest of lies but felt it was necessary in this case.

"Let me know if he tries to contact you again, okay?"

"Why? Is there something I should know about him?" I waited with bated breath after I said those words.

He stood up from the chair and looked down at me. His facial expression changed from one of relief to one I couldn't quite pinpoint, and that was frightening.

"The Cross family owns this town. Nothing gets past them in this city and if you want to do certain things, they need to approve it first. They are known to dabble into dangerous things, although there has been no legitimate proof that has been brought to the authorities. Hell, it might have been, but they probably have all of them in their back pockets anyway."

A quiver ran down my back as his words. My gut told me I should be afraid, but having it confirmed was another matter entirely. I needed to find out more, but I wasn't sure how most of the things I wanted to know might be completely scrubbed from the Internet. Another thought popped into my head. "Is that why you went to them to bail the company out instead of going to a bank?"

"In part, yes. I looked into several loans and none of them would have expedited the amount we needed as quickly as we needed it."

Part of me wondered if that had anything to do with Damien, but I didn't want to raise my father's suspicions about what Damien and I were doing. But this was something I needed to know. "Dad, what dangerous things has the Cross family done?"

He shifted his weight and ran a hand through his short-cropped hair and then he replied, "There have been talks of potential ties to the Mafia. Not that they're in it, but they might have some dealings with them."

I kept my face unreadable. "And I'm willing to bet it was swept under the rug, right?"

My father nodded. "Be careful, Anais. If Damien contacts you, let me know, okay?"

Not sure what you could do even if we weren't sleeping together. "I will, Dad."

"I love you and we should try to go out to dinner with your mother sometime soon, okay?"

"Okay, and I love you, too."

Once he left and closed the door behind him, I threw my head into my hands, wondering what I had gotten myself into.

16

DAMIEN

"Melissa, I'm going to need those files from Samson after this meeting."

"I'm on it, Mr. Cross." I said nothing else as we walked toward the conference room door, so Melissa continued, "Don't forget you have 2 p.m. and a 3:15."

I checked my watch. Ten minutes until the meeting. I nodded and she started to walk away before she turned back to me. "Thanks for the fruit basket."

I was taken aback by her comment, but I didn't show it. It took a second then it clicked about what she was talking about. "Happy birthday." I'd made a standing order with a local company to send Melissa a fruit basket for her birthday every year.

She smiled at me and walked away again, I assumed back to her desk, which was stationed right outside of my office. I walked into the conference room and grabbed a seat near the door.

"How are things going with the woman of the hour?"

"What are you talking about?"

I didn't even bother to look at Gage as I patiently waited for the meeting to begin. My father, brothers, myself, and other staff were coordinating to have a plan ready to go for one of the biggest board meetings that Cross Industries had ever seen. Hence the need to make sure we were aptly prepared for just about anything that might happen or any question that might come up.

"We already know that the woman we saw draped in gold at Elevate the last time you were there is now living in your townhouse," Broderick chimed in from across the table.

I saw Gage sit up in his chair out of the corner of my eye. "You moved her into your townhouse too?"

"Are you all done?"

"They better be because we have work to do."

All eyes were on Dad as he walked into the conference room shutting down the conversation. It was rare that I heard Dad use a tone that reminded me of how he used to talk to us when we were children doing something that we had no business doing. Clearly, that tone was still effective because we all fixed our postures to get ready for the meeting. It didn't take long for the senior staff to file in. The meeting started and my mind was focused on all things related to our business ventures.

When it was getting closer to the end, my thoughts turned to Anais staying at my home and keeping my dick wet. Due to our busy schedules, we didn't get to spend much time together.

"Mr. Cross?"

The meeting had just wrapped up. Everyone swung around to face the voice since they didn't know which Cross Melissa was talking to.

"I, uh, meant Damien." She looked somewhat surprised that she had said my first name. "There is someone here to see you."

I stood up and walked over to her. "Who is here to see me?"

"She said her name was Anais Monroe. Said you would know who she is."

I checked my phone to see if she had left a message, but I didn't see one. *She pulled this off as a surprise. Interesting.*

"Did I do the wrong thing? She's sitting in the lobby."

I glanced at Melissa after I put away my phone. "No, what you did was fine. I'll take care of it."

I excused myself from the conference room without causing a fuss and headed toward the lobby. It didn't take me long to spot Anais sitting in the first row of chairs closest to the door. By the look on her face, she was pissed. I took my time to appreciate her coming to my office in a red pencil skirt. She was also wearing those "fuck me" beige pumps that she had worn the first time we met.

"Ms. Monroe." She looked up at me and the look in her eye told me this was going to be a fun meeting. "Please follow me to my office."

I placed a hand on the small of her back and guided her through the cubicles on my floor. I could see everyone's eyes avoiding mine, but I knew they were watching as we marched to my office. I was glad that my brothers were either still in the conference room or had gone to their own floors to manage their operations because I would never hear the end of this, and it was the last thing I needed. I could feel my subordinates' ache to gossip about the scene that was occurring in front of them and I knew they would once we were out of sight. Not that I never had business associates come to my office to hold meetings, but she was different. The energy around us was different and I understood why it would send tongues around us wagging.

The walk to my office ended with me closing my office door. "To what do I owe this pleasure?"

She seemed stunned as she took in the room. I will admit that my office was pretty remarkable. It was located in one of the corners of the floor and had large windows that allowed me to look at the tall skyscrapers featured in New York City's skyline whenever I wanted. I had a big-screen TV on one wall in case I wanted to watch the news or the stock exchange. The other walls featured charitable and business accolades. While she was caught trying to take in as much of my office as she could, my mind drifted to visions of her bent over my desk. That was when she snapped out of it and turned her attention back to me with fire burning in her eyes.

"What the hell do you think you're doing?"

"What are you talking about?"

"Did you tell my father that we were doing whatever this is?"

What the hell was this about? "No. I had a phone call with your father about the loan and we may have a meeting later this week. You were not brought up at all."

"Did you have someone send him a photo of us from Elevate?"

"I wouldn't lower myself to leak a photo. Elevate has strict security protocols and you're saying someone disobeyed my rules?" Someone had the audacity to not only leak a photo from Elevate, they leaked a photo of Anais and me? The anger that her accusation and a leak in my club caused in me went unchecked. How dare she think that I would do such a thing? Before she responded, I continued. "An investigation into who took the picture will occur. Never accuse me of going back on my word. We had an agreement and I've kept my word."

I checked my wrist again. I had less than ten minutes until my next meeting. There wasn't enough time to bend her over my desk now but there was always next time.

She snorted. "I can't trust you. You lie to people all the time."

I got close to her and tilted her chin up to force her to look me in the eye. "I have never lied to you and I never will."

She said nothing, and I wasn't sure that she accepted what I said or not.

"Here I thought you were just here to get fucked across my desk."

Her eyes darted from the desk and back to me. "This isn't about sex. This is about my father suspecting that there is something up between us and it's something I didn't want him to know."

"It had to have been someone you know that told him."

"How dare you attempt to accuse Ellie!"

I locked the door behind me, a decisive click letting both of us know what had been done. "I didn't accuse anyone. I know that my people keep their mouths shut and have sworn their loyalty. It sounds like there might be a problem on your end that needs to be solved. We'll get to the bottom of who is attempting to leak this." I took a step toward her forcing her to back up. I did it again and again and again until she was up against my desk. "This isn't really an issue, that you're linked to me. You're already mine."

And that was when my lips slammed down on hers. The kiss turned serious fast and it was intoxicating. I broke it to whisper to her, "Place your hands on the edge of my desk and don't move."

She did as I said without argument and I growled in satisfaction. *Thank fuck because I don't have time to waste anyway.*

My mouth usually went to her neck first, to the spot that I found that drove her wild, but I mixed it up. My eyes zeroed in on her tits that were currently hiding from me behind a bra and white shirt. How had I still not gotten enough of them? "Unbutton the shirt now or I'll rip it off you myself."

Once again, she followed directions and soon she was standing in front of me in her lacy beige bra, her shirt falling off her shoulders, and her mouth slightly open, her breath coming out in light pants. Her green eyes told me that she was waiting to see what I was going to do next.

My mouth made its way to her breast licking a small trail along the top of it, while my hand massaged the other because it deserved some attention as well. When I heard a moan escape her lips, my dick stiffened in my pants and I was already regretting not being able to put it in her tight pussy due to this meeting that could have taken place over an email.

After my tongue made its way to the start of her cleavage, I used my other hand to yank that bra cup down and put her light brown nipple into my mouth. I glanced up and watched as she threw her head back and let out a groan, not caring who could walk by and hear her. A minute later, I moved onto her other breast, paying as much attention to it as I did the previous one. I loved to hear the sounds that were coming out of her mouth as she lost her mind because of what I was doing to her. When I was done, I let her nipple out of my mouth with a loud pop and knelt to get ready to go toward the main course of this meal.

"Remember what I said. Don't move your hands away from the desk or I'll stop."

She nodded her head, but words were past her at this point as she didn't say anything, but her breathing became more erratic the lower I went.

"I can't wait to get my mouth on this pretty pussy." I glanced up at her and found her eyeing me as I pushed her skirt up and shifted her panties to the side and touched her folds with my fingers as she shuddered. "You're already wet for me and I've only just begun."

I pulled two of the chairs that that were sitting in front of my desk a little bit closer and she intuitively knew to put her heels up on the chairs and that's when I submerged myself into her and she told me that I had done the right thing when she bucked forward, but I held steady and reached around to grab her ass, making sure there was no way she was getting away from my mouth.

Part of me wanted her to thread her fingers through my hair just so I could punish her when we got home, but so far, she was doing her damnedest to keep her fingers clutched tight on the desk, honoring what I'd told her earlier. My tongue made its way to her clit and even if I didn't know I'd made the right decision, her body would have told me I did based on the cuss words she was spewing. Her taste was sweet, something that I could see myself wanting to have for the rest of my days although I knew that couldn't be.

I switched between sucking and licking, not sticking to a particular rhythm so she didn't know what was coming next and I could feel her losing control of her body. The harder her breaths became, the harder my motions, and when I felt her fingers in my hair, I hid my grin. *I got another thing I wanted.*

"Damien." My name came out as a groan and I almost moaned too. I knew I would never tire of that sound and I continued consuming her as if I needed her to live.

A few more seconds and she fell apart and I licked every drop of her, enjoying the taste of her in my mouth. When I pulled back, she looked as if she had been properly fucked with her tits on display and her pussy still glistening from the havoc I had just wreaked on it.

I sat back on my heels and then I stood up, pulling my suit jacket down to cover my dick, which was now at full mast. I checked my watch and bit back a cuss. This had taken eight minutes instead of seven.

"I have a two o'clock and need to head out. Stay in here as long as you need. I'll see you at home later." I paused for a moment. "Take your time too because you look as if you've been properly fucked."

I gave her a small smirk before I exited my office, closing the door behind me.

17
ANAIS

"We can talk about this later."

"Sounds good, Jake," I said as I walked into my office and closed the door. I eased down into my chair, finally able to show that I sore show all over my face after Damien had taken me this morning. I was just about to make a phone call when my phone buzzed alerting me that I had a text message.

Damien: *Be ready to go by 7. Rob will pick you up from home.*

I closed my eyes, first trying to calm myself to tame the urge to send a snarky text message. It would have been nice if he'd asked me if I had any plans. I also would have appreciated more than a few hours' heads-up that I had to go somewhere. There was also the fact that he called his townhouse home to me, when previously he'd always referred to it as "my home." Could be a slip of the fingers, but when has Damien ever slipped up? Before I could analyze it any further, a second text message from Damien popped up on my phone.

Damien: *Don't worry about picking out something. I had my stylist send a few options.*

I furiously typed a message back to him.

Me: *No. I'm not going.*

Damien: *Yes, you are.*

Me: *I don't get a say in this? Shocking. Could you have given me more than a few hours' heads-up? I don't want it to leak that we were seen together and have it get back to my father.*

I pressed send and placed my phone face down on my desk. A frustrated growl escaped my mouth after I checked the time. It was almost four, which meant I should start wrapping up things here soon in order to get back to the townhouse to be ready in just a few short hours. My phone buzzed again.

Damien: *My father was supposed to go to this event but can't and asked me to take his place instead. We could entertain each other.*

Well, at least he too had found out last minute. That lessened some of the anger that I felt. I noticed he hadn't said anything about news about us being revealed to the press. I was worried about more photos leaking and my father finding out that I lied by omission, but I didn't push it further.

Me: *Could you at least tell me what this event is about? That might help me decide on an outfit that's appropriate.*

Damien: *It's a cocktail and dinner event. I have to make an appearance and act friendly.*

Me: *Act is right. You mean until you take over their companies and portfolios?*

Damien: *You got it. Rob will get you from work at 4:45. You will be ready to go by 7.*

∼

THE RIDE to Damien's took longer than usual with traffic factored in, but I made it there with plenty of time to spare. I jumped into the shower but avoided wetting my hair in order to save time. When I got out, I noticed a black off-the-shoulder cocktail dress, a dark red sheath dress that dipped a bit in the front, and a long-sleeved forest-green boatneck sheath dress hanging on a small rack in the bedroom. On the floor near the foot of the bed were black pumps and I was thankful that at least they were basic, and I didn't have to make a choice between shoes as well. They hadn't been there before I entered the shower, making me wonder who had left them. If it had been Damien, I was shocked he didn't stop by the bathroom to see me, assuming he didn't let the stylist come into my bedroom. Knowing that it was December, I walked into the closet that was filled to brim with expensive clothes, wondering what the reason was for asking his stylist to bring clothes when I could have found something suitable. I found a beautiful long white peacoat and placed it on the bed next to the forest-green dress I decided to wear tonight.

It didn't take me long to put my dress on and apply my makeup. I thought about spending some time putting my hair up but kept it down for the sake of convenience. As I finished putting on my heels, there was a knock on the door.

"Come in," I said and was shocked to find Damien on the other side of the door. He had knocked instead of barging into the room? Was I living in an alternate universe? He was focused on how tight the dress was in the bodice area before his eyes made their way down the rest of my body to stare at my legs.

He liked what he saw although he said nothing about my appearance.

"Wear these," he said as he handed me a small box.

My heart temporarily jumped into my mouth because of its shape, but my brain finally caught up to my eyes and noticed that it was too big to hold a ring. When I opened the box, I found a pair of rectangular-cut diamond and emerald earrings. On top was a diamond and dangling from it was an emerald.

I almost slammed the box shut and dropped it.

"You want to ask a question."

"Whatever could have given you that idea?"

"Because you never shut up."

I couldn't tell if he meant that as a compliment or an insult, but I took it as the former.

"How much did this cost?"

"That's not important. It's a gift."

"Will this be added to my debt?"

His eyes flared. "What part of 'it's a gift' don't you understand?"

Was giving earrings that were probably worth more than what I had in my savings account just an everyday occurrence for him?

"Why did you buy them?"

"Because they reminded me of your eyes. If you hadn't picked the green dress to wear, I hoped these might have convinced you otherwise."

I had nothing else to say and although I felt uncomfortable wearing something so expensive, in the back of my mind, I knew part of my job tonight was to be a representation of him and all of the companies that were a part of the

"Cross Empire," so I put the earrings on. I could talk to him about not being able to accept these later.

I put on the white coat and grabbed the black purse that I was going to be using for the night. When I looked at him, he nodded, turned around to walk out of my room, and waited in the hallway. I checked my makeup one more time and I followed behind him, closing the door on my way out. We waited for the elevator to take us down to the main level and when we reached the front door, he held out his arm for me to grab as we descended the front porch stairs where Rob was waiting with our ride. Damien waited for me to enter the sedan before walking around the car to enter on the other side.

"Is everything okay?" His actions raised my bullshit meter and I wanted to know what this was all about.

He didn't say anything, but he looked at me.

"You're acting like a gentleman and I want to know what's up."

"Are you questioning me?"

"No." I thought about arguing further but figured if I wanted to have a nice evening tonight, it wouldn't be worth what this was about to turn into.

As he said, the ride to the event was short and I clutched Damien's arm as we made our way through the crowd of people that were in attendance. We were gathering in the enormous living room of someone who had more money than I could ever imagine. I could see what looked to be part of a large, stunning staircase down into the hall.

Almost as soon as we arrived, everyone wanted to talk to Damien and therefore me since I was on his arm. While people were talking to him, I watched as Damien's eyes scanned the room. What he was looking for, I didn't know. I prayed that this wouldn't get back to my father, but if it did, what good was it worrying about it now? What was done was done.

I felt my body tense up, and Damien must have sensed it too because he rubbed his hand up and down the small of my back, providing a small sense of comfort in the very crowded room in an unfamiliar place.

"Damien, hello!"

Although we were in the middle of a conversation, this man, whose name I didn't catch, had to let his presence be known. Damien's eyes narrowed. He was supposedly talking to Damien, but his eyes were zeroed in on me. "Take your eyes off of her if you ever want to breathe, let alone work in this city again."

Damien's words sent a tremble down my spine. The people in our immediate vicinity heard Damien's words and either took a small step back or looked at him with wide eyes. I did neither of those things because I suspected something like that might come out of his mouth based on the irritation he had with this guy and his hand, which had been on my lower back, had now moved to my waist, holding me to him like a vise. All this man did was look at me and that was enough to make Damien go off. I refused to admit to Damien or anyone else how much it aroused me.

The man in question got the message quickly and his attention was on Damien before finding an excuse to leave us alone. I was relieved because I truly thought Damien might kill him.

I leaned over to whisper in Damien's ear. "Was that really necessary?"

"What did I say about questioning me? I didn't like how he was looking at what was mine and I let it be known. End of discussion."

The conversations continued until at one point, Damien excused both of us and pulled me away to where we could be alone.

"Do you want to get a drink or anything?"

I thought about it for a moment and said, "I think I'm going to go with water."

"Not Merlot?"

I snorted. "Trying to keep a clear mind instead of drinking and turning into a lush."

"Damien, long time no see."

Damien and I turned to find a tall, tan-skinned man standing behind us. His aura was off-putting. I looked at the stranger in front of me and then back up at Damien. It was clear as day that this individual was no stranger to Damien.

"Will. It's good to see you." Damien's tone said that it was anything but.

I knew my instincts were correct.

"Likewise."

"I just wanted to come over and say hello after I saw you across the room." His eyes turned to me and he said, "And you are?"

I hesitated for a moment before I said, "Anais."

"Well. What a beautiful name for a beautiful woman."

I thought about rolling my eyes at his very cliché comment, but something told me that wouldn't go over well. Who was he?

"I'll let you get back to it. It was nice seeing you again."

"Likewise," Damien replied.

When Will left, I turned to Damien and asked, "Who was that?"

"Just someone I knew a long time ago. You don't have to worry about him."

Although I didn't think that was the end of it, his voice, thick with assertiveness, was reassuring and it scared me.

18

ANAIS

"Damien, I don't think I'm properly dressed for an evening at Elevate."

"It doesn't matter what you look like since you're with me."

I rolled my eyes and threw my head back onto the headrest. I knew Elevate would be fun, I just also knew I was overdressed no matter how much Damien said I wasn't, but I was ready for a more relaxed vibe after spending most of my evening at a function I didn't care to be at. But had the security issue been taken care of? It irritated me because I kept thinking about it, but I didn't want to deal with the fallout from it.

"But—" I leaned forward to argue with him because this was a terrible idea.

"The security issue is being handled and the majority of people that will be there tonight won't see you."

I sat back because he ripped the wind from my sails when he answered my question.

It didn't take long for us to arrive, but we drove past the

entrance. The SUV turned down an alleyway and we were escorted into the building through a door behind the building. Damien led the way as we went up to the VIP lounge where we were seated and given drinks.

"Not too bad, huh?" Damien asked as he dipped his head to whisper in my ear.

I shook my head. "No, this is great. I don't know if I've ever been in the VIP portion of a bar or club."

"Well, there is always a first time for everything."

The way he said those words both aroused and frustrated me. Ellie's words about becoming addicted to Damien replayed in my mind. I closed my eyes briefly, tossing her words aside because there was nothing wrong with enjoying how he made my body feel. No emotions required.

"We're going downstairs tonight."

"I uh — wasn't expecting that." I wasn't opposed to it and the thought of trying something new with him down there was more than enough to get me excited. I had just thought we might get a quick drink and head home. Visions of what he might have planned flashed through my mind. If he brought up anything outside of what I was comfortable with I was walking out.

"You should always expect the unexpected, especially when it comes to me. We'll head down after you finish your drink." His eyes dared me to fight him on it, but I didn't want to.

What I wanted to do was continue to press his buttons and I did that by drinking my drink even slower than normal.

I could see him growing impatient while I cradled my drink, determined to draw this out as long as possible. I stood up and walked over to the balcony. I sipped from my drink and looked out at the crowd. The atmosphere in the club was electric and part of me wished I was partaking in the festivities below. The VIP area was secluded from the rest of the night life, making me feel both envied and envious.

"Let's head downstairs," he said as I took another sip of my drink.

I hadn't heard him walk over nor had I felt his presence, so his voice caused a small tremble. "I haven't finished my drink yet."

"I'll get you another."

His annoyance with my stalling was obvious. I swallowed a mouthful of the liquid left in my glass, polishing it off. My attempts to stop the inevitable were over.

It was now or never. Damien grabbed my hand and together we walked down the stairs and came face-to-face with a security guard. This time I had no problem getting in with Damien leading the way.

Damien led me down a dark hallway and the first stop on the tour was a lounge that looked like the bar upstairs, but the vibe was different. The energy was more sensual and pure sex. Although there were couches in the large room, most people were on the dance floor grinding on one another and having a great time. The lack of clothing helped set the mood as I watched a woman in what I would call a dominatrix outfit lead a man, who was just in his boxers, around on a chain.

I leaned forward and asked Damien, "Would you ever let me take charge like that?"

The look he gave me told me what I needed to know, and I bit my lip as we walked past a gigantic room that seemed to go on forever.

Bang. I jumped several inches in the air at the loud noise that came from my right. The noise came from a woman who was now leaning up against a glass door that looked out into the hallway we were walking down. Her hands and breasts were plastered against the door as her partner appeared from the shadows and started fucking her from behind.

It was Damien's turn to whisper in my ear. "I can tell by your reaction you wish that was you."

"It was also a sudden loud noise."

"Uh-huh." He didn't believe me, and I didn't believe myself. The look of pure ecstasy on the woman's face said it all. "Maybe you'll be interested in some of the other themed rooms."

"It's up to you since you control my pleasure."

"Now you're starting to get it." The look he gave me when he said those words had me ready to confess every secret I had as long as it led to him giving me that look and so much more. We continued down the hall, passing a few play areas including one that was safari themed and another that had a nautical theme. When we passed a room that was dressed in different variations of red lights, almost painting the picture of flames being on the walls, I noticed Damien visibly stiffen, but before I could ask, he was pulling me toward a door.

"Here we are," Damien said. We walked inside and he closed the door behind us. The room he picked was much more like what I deemed to be his personality. He chose a dimly lit room, whose light was coming from a fake fireplace. The king-size bed in the middle of the room was the only other thing that I could see. "Strip. Down to your bra and panties."

Normally I had no problem arguing with him, but the

darkness of his tone sent a shiver down my spine that I tried to hide. I didn't want him to know the effect that he was having on me out of fear that he might use it against me. "You're going to have to unzip me."

I turned around and pulled up my hair giving him plenty of room to maneuver. He placed his hands on my thighs and they drifted up my sides, where he briefly touched my breasts before moving his hands toward my back. He slowly unzipped my dress and when it was about halfway down, I let my hair down, allowing it to swing loosely down my back. His quick intake of breath told me he enjoyed that image. I dragged the green sleeves off my shoulders, allowing the dress to gather at my waist.

I wore a black lacy bra and panties under my dress. It had been a splurge purchase about four months ago and I finally wore it tonight, to give me some more confidence. It somewhat worked, or maybe it was the drink I had. He was enjoying what I was wearing although it wasn't for him.

I rolled my eyes before I stopped moving an idea formed in my mind. Damien loved being several steps ahead, but I wondered if I could get the upper hand here. I slowly unzipped the dress and made a bit of a show of getting the tight dress off of my body by bending down, letting him see all of my cleavage as I dragged the dress over my waist and down my legs.

"You think this act is cute?" His voice came out a little hoarse, so I knew my "act" had done what I intended it to do. "You're not in control here. I am."

"There is one thing I am in control of. We haven't talked about any boundaries and I want to clarify that I'm not doing anything that I'm not comfortable with. If it pisses you off, so be it."

His eyes narrowed and then a smirk appeared on his lips. "I was waiting to see if you would say something. You always have a choice." With those words, he backed me up against the wall and I loved the sensation of the cool wall against my warm back.

"What do you want?"

His question startled me for a split second. I answered honestly. "You. I want you."

"Undress me."

Feeling bold, I didn't hesitate to reach for his pants, wanting to take his cock out. I took my time unbuttoning his shirt and once all of the buttons were done, I peeled the shirt off, removing it from the hard muscles on his shoulders and down his arms before I threw it on the floor. I bit my lip as I undid his pants' button, unzipped his fly, and unbuckled his belt and watched his pants fall down, leaving a pool of cloth at his feet. He quickly removed them along with his shoes and socks. I couldn't help but stare at his perfect form before our eyes met. The desire that flashed in his eyes made me even more wet as I looked at his hard abs and the black boxer briefs that he had on. I felt as if his bulge was teasing me, and I couldn't wait for him to fuck me. No emotions, just pleasure.

"I shouldn't want this," Damien murmured as he lifted my head with both hands and kissed me. My senses went on overload as his desperation seeped through. The kiss became more wicked and his hands left my face and made their way down my neck and to my breasts. He was the first to break the kiss and launched an attack of kissing and sucking on my neck. I expected him to work his magic there, but he switched it up on me when he pulled back and bent down, wrapping his hands around my legs, and pulling them around his waist. I wasn't expecting the motion and I squealed in response. When I looked at Damien, I saw a hint of a smile on his lips.

He carried me across the room and gently tossed me on the bed. "You know, it's been a while since I heard you say anything, Spitfire. Let's turn this up a notch."

He peeled my bra straps down my shoulders and my tits sprang free from their enclosure. I heard him groan under his breath, trying to keep a lid on his yearning for me. Looked like all of this was turning things up a notch for him instead of me. That was until his lips landed on my breasts. When his mouth met my nipples I moaned, mentally acknowledging that he had turned the tables. He worshipped my breasts as if they were everything he needed to survive and slowly his hand made its way down my body. When he touched my pussy, I was ready to drag his cock inside me. He pulled back and looked down at me, his eyes moving between where his fingers lay and my eyes.

"Who made you this wet?"

Forming words wasn't on my agenda so I didn't make a peep, even fighting back the moan that was dancing in my throat.

"Anais." His voice was low and full of warning. "I'll move my hand."

"No! Fuck! I'm wet because of you."

"Good answer." With that, his finger slipped between my folds and I let out the moan that I had been fighting for what seemed like forever. How was I already revving up to come this quickly?

His fingers moved in and out of me with a finesse that

none of the men I had been with previously had. When he added another finger, it didn't take long for me to soar above the imaginary clouds that had formed in my mind. I rode out my orgasm on his fingers and when he removed his fingers my orgasm was cruising back down in altitude. I thought he would give me a breather, but he wasn't done yet.

"Get on your knees. Put your fingers on that cunt while I get ready."

My body moved on reflex and I found myself on all fours on the soft king-size bed. I felt empowered as my fingers rubbed my clit and I could feel his eyes zeroed in on the motions that my hand was doing as I pleasured myself. I heard the ripping of the condom wrapper.

"You don't know how much I love this ass," Damien murmured as I heard him get closer to me.

Not being able to see him heightened my other senses and I almost buckled when I felt his dick teasing my entrance. I loved when he ran his cock up and down my seam, because I never knew when he would enter me. He did it repeatedly and I wondered if he was waiting on me to beg. He wasn't.

He entered me and I whimpered, feeling relieved that he finally satiated my need to have him inside of me. Him entering me from behind was a novel experience and the sensations that Damien set off in my body as he fucked me took me to another planet. His pace quickened and it didn't take long for the first smack to land on my ass. The sting from the hit sent another load of pleasure through my body and got me closer to my second orgasm. When he did it two more times, I could feel myself about to take the deep dive once again.

With a few longer strokes, I cried out, reaching the tipping point. Damien didn't let up the pace until he succumbed to his own orgasm after I had. He collapsed on my back, removing himself from me. Damien got up to head to the bathroom, leaving me alone in the room. Although I knew I could feel safe in this place, my gut told me that danger wasn't too far away.

19

ANAIS

I looked down an aisle and didn't see what I wanted, so I moved on to the next. I made an impulsive trip to a drug store near my office after work to grab a couple of things before heading back to Damien's. I saw the aisle that was full of nail care items and hurried to pick out a new nail polish color. Smiling when I found the one, I plucked the container off the rack and placed it in the basket I was holding. The deep brown that I found was a perfect color for winter.

I headed toward the front and got in a small line that had gathered near the cash registers. I zoned out for a moment, wondering what I was going to do for the rest of the night.

"Thank you. Have a good evening."

My head shot up not just because I was next in line but because of the voice I just heard. Why was it familiar? I looked to my left and noticed a man with a black hoodie and baseball cap walking away.

That was when it dawned on me. The scratchy voice was

similar to the man who shoulder-checked me outside of my apartment before this deal with Damien began. I hurried to the register and tossed my things on the counter with a tight smile. I hoped that the sales associate in front of me would have no issues ringing up my purchases because I needed to find this guy.

Thankfully, the clerk had me out within a couple of minutes.

I knew better than to confront him by myself because I didn't know what type of danger that posed, but I wanted to get a good look at him. There was no way I was going to believe that it was just a coincidence that he walked into the same drug store as me. I rushed toward the front door and the cold air hit me like a slap in the face. After looking up and down the street several times, I couldn't find him. The person that was following me was still out there and I couldn't do anything about it. I snatched my phone from out of my bag and called the first person who came to mind.

"Anais."

Just him saying my name helped warm me against the cold that was caused by the chill of the wind and the fear in my soul. "Are you at your place?"

"I'm a few minutes away. Why?"

"I think I'm being followed. Can you stay on the phone with me until I get to your place?" The confident mask I usually wore around Damien was cracked.

"Where are you?" His no-nonsense tone soothed me a bit and I hated to admit it.

"Two blocks away from your house."

"You'll get there first because of traffic. When you arrive, lock the doors until I get there. I'll stay on the line until you do."

I sighed. What could we talk about? "Tell me a funny story." I looked over my shoulder but found nothing out of the ordinary.

He didn't miss a beat. "One memory that I have from childhood is that I was in the living room finishing my homework with my mom helping me. I couldn't have been more than six at the time. With three boys under the age of seven in her house, she knew that something was up when things were a bit too quiet. She found my twin brothers playing in her makeup when they were around two or three. I remember the horrified scream she let out."

I snorted. "I'm sure she wasn't too thrilled to have to clean them up." I felt some relief wash over me when I spotted Damien's house in the distance.

"Nope, but I couldn't lie and say that I wasn't happy that they were getting in trouble."

The small amount of glee in his voice made me smile as I walked up the stairs to Damien's place, almost forgetting the reason that I called him.

∼

I COULD FEEL myself waking up even though my body was telling me it wasn't time to do so yet because I was still exhausted. After talking with Damien and discussing my potentially using Rob to go to and from work I came up to my room and went to bed early.

A low beeping noise was playing, but I couldn't tell if it was something in my dream or in real life. It took another second for me to become fully awake and to sit up in bed. I heard the door creak and I turned and found that Damien was in my room. I scrambled to get out of the covers and when I looked at him, he put a finger to his lips, letting me know that I should be quiet. I reached over and pulled a hoodie on over my tank top and sweatpants.

"What's going on?" I whispered, fumbling to fix the clothes on my body.

He didn't answer right away, and my eyes widened until he held up one finger. That was when I realized he was attempting to listen for any strange noises. Did this have anything to do with the low beeping noise I'd heard earlier?

"Someone is attempting to enter the house and tripped the alarm."

I listened once more, and I heard the beeps sound a couple more times and then they stopped. He pulled out his phone and opened up what looked to be an app, but I didn't recognize the icon.

"Come with me," he said, and I dashed over to him. He wrapped his arm around my waist, and his bare arm on the small of my back provided some of the warmth that I didn't know I wanted.

He guided me out of my bedroom and quietly up the stairs. He stopped in front of a closed door and I held my breath when I realized he had led me to his bedroom. With one swipe of his phone, he opened the door.

Given the situation and the lack of lighting, I didn't take the time to look around the room like I had wanted to. I watched as he walked over to a corner, guided by the light from his phone, and placed his fingers just under the tabletop of his desk. I took a step toward him, not totally understanding what he was doing, and a beat later I heard a door open on the other side of the room.

He rushed back over to me and said, "Anais. Listen to me. This is not the time to argue with me. I want you to head over to that corner of the room and go through the door. The door will close behind you and I need you to stay put until I can get you."

I nodded and followed Damien back toward the open door.

"Rob has called in reinforcements and this is just a precaution."

I nodded again and walked through the door, not sure what might meet me on the other side. When I walked in, an overhead light turned on. I glanced around before turning to Damien.

"I'll be back as soon as I can. If I'm not back in fifteen minutes, use either that phone or that panic button under the desk to call the police." He pointed to a black phone that looked to be connected to a landline in the corner.

I moved my head so I could see the circular red button on the underside of the desk. "Okay."

Damien gave me one last look before he left, closing the door behind him, and encapsulating me inside. I took a deep breath and turned around to continue examining my surroundings. I found a storage container full of dried food and water. Another contained at least two first aid kits, blankets, clothes, flashlights, hand crank radio, portable toilet, and toilet paper. The final container had what looked to be cards, a portable chess set, and a couple of other things to serve as a way to pass the time. Essentially, there was anything and everything that you would need to survive for several weeks in this room.

Damien had taken a lot of thought in putting these materials in this room and had made sure that whoever was in here would be prepared for just about any instance, that was for sure. And that feeling helped calm my nerves temporarily. I patted my body, trying to find my phone, and realized I had left it in my bedroom.

"Fuck," I muttered as I debated what I could do. I reached into the bin and took out the cards and started dealing them out to play a round of solitaire. It wasn't how I thought I'd be spending my Wednesday night when I should have been sleeping.

As the game went on, I noticed that my hands were becoming clammy, although I was in a cool room. I checked the clock on the wall and if it was correct, only seven minutes had passed, so I continued playing.

A couple of minutes later, I heard a slam that nearly caused me to jump out of my skin. "What the hell was that?"

Of course, silence answered my question as I stood up and walked over to the door. I hoped that Damien, Rob, and whoever their backup was would be okay. I placed my ear against it for a few seconds and I realized that wasn't a good idea because if someone started shooting, I would more than likely get hit by a bullet. With that thought in my mind, I backed away quickly until my back reached the other wall. It didn't take long for any lasting confidence that I had to fall by the wayside and the sense of dread to creep into my veins. Sweat broke out over my skin, causing me to tremble for a moment. When the tightness in my chest started, it finally clicked what was happening: panic attack. I slid down on the wall in a fetal position on the hard, wooden floor.

I hadn't had a panic attack like this since I was a teenager, right before I had to present a group project in biology. Now was definitely not a good time to be having one.

I tried to take deep breaths to at least ease the tightness in my chest, but it wasn't doing much to help. The nausea that rolled in soon after was interfering with my breathing, causing me to struggle even more. The tears increased and were free flowing down my face and although I tried to keep somewhat quiet, I knew I was failing.

I didn't know how long I was in that position, but seconds turned into minutes that then turned into what felt like hours as I waited for someone to free me from this room.

"Get it together," I tried to tell myself and that lessened my tears some. I slowed my heart rate down to a point that I could force myself to crawl over to the desk and looked up at the clock on the wall.

"Three minutes to go," I muttered to myself and pulled open some of the drawers, thinking that maybe looking through them would take my mind off of what was going on in the house. I found some papers in the top drawer, but I didn't have time to read them. I opened the bottom drawer, and my eyes widened. A gun was staring back at me. I pulled it out of the drawer and wondered why Damien hadn't mentioned that it was in here. I studied it for a minute before placing it on top of the desk. This might come in handy in case someone tried to break into the panic room. The only problem was that I'd never fired a gun, so I hoped the safety wasn't on so that if I needed to, I could just pull the trigger and ask questions later. I'd deal with whether or not I could pull the trigger if the time came.

I had so many questions that needed answering, but there were several that stood out to me. Who the hell would break into Damien's house? And why did he find it necessary to install a panic room in his home?

20

ANAIS

Just as I got up to make the phone call, I heard the creaking of a floorboard outside. My feelings jumped from being terrified to attempting to calm myself in order to think rationally. I heard another creaky board bow under the pressure of someone's weight and that caused me to get into position. I snatched the gun and flicked the lights off and bent down, crouching down in front of a counter.

"Anais?"

My name came off his lips in a hushed whisper. But that was all I needed to restore a sense of calm. In my mind, we were safe.

I backed away as the door opened, dropping the gun at my feet. Damien sprinted inside.

"You're all right."

"Yes," he responded and then he acted as if he was checking me for bruises, as if I was the one who had just gone out to face whoever had tried to break into his home. "Are you okay?"

"A little shaken up, but I'm fine."

"You're not fine. You look as if you've been crying." He wiped the remaining tears from my face. "Whoever sent that asshole to my house is going to pay for putting those tears in your eyes."

"With everything going on—" I was staring at his face until I noticed a small red smear on his cheek. "Is that blood?"

I moved to take a closer look and that was when I finally got a look at his hands.

"Damien, your hands are bleeding."

"It's not mine. You need to pack a bag." He didn't hide the fact that he was changing the subject.

"Wait, what?"

"We're getting out of here," he said, getting ready to pull me along behind him, but I pulled my hand back.

"What do you mean we're leaving? We should probably call the cops and wait for them to get here."

He shook his head. "Don't worry about the police. Pack your duffle bag with a few essentials and the rest can wait until we get there."

"Get where?"

"Anais, right now is not the time to be asking a million questions. Just do as I say. Rob should be standing outside your door just in case."

"What are you going to do?"

"I'm packing as well."

I nodded and Damien walked me to the stairs. Sure enough, Rob was standing at the bottom close enough to guard my bedroom door, so I sprinted down the stairs. Rob gave me a slight nod as I entered, and I packed up as much as I could before Damien appeared back at my door.

"Are you set?"

"Give me one second." I threw on a sweatshirt that I had brought from my apartment and grabbed a thick winter coat from the closet. "Yes, now I am."

"Okay. Let's move."

When we made our way downstairs, another man that I swore I had seen previously was standing near the sink washing his hands.

"Kingston, we are going to head out now."

Kingston turned around as he was drying his hands and looked at both of us. That's when it hit me. "You're the security guard from Elevate."

"I am. I'm also Damien's cousin."

"Oh lovely, there are more of you Crosses in the world." Watching Kingston dry his hands triggered another memory as I looked at Damien's face and hands. The only thing that told me that he might have gotten into a scuffle was the bruising that stained his knuckles.

The men chuckled. "We need to get a move on," Damien said and faced Kingston. "If you hear anything, let me know."

Kingston nodded and said, "You know I will. It was nice seeing you again, Anais."

I was shocked that he knew my name. "Likewise."

Damien and Rob grabbed the bags and I followed them out to an awaiting SUV. I found a couple more men that I had never seen before standing with their guns drawn. "What the hell?" But no one said anything as we got into the SUV and it took off into the dark of night.

I turned to Damien, who was busy on his phone next to me and hadn't said a word since we left his home.

"Is now a good time to ask questions?" I couldn't believe how meek my voice sounded and Damien must have thought the same because when he looked up, I saw a hint of concern in his eyes and his expression.

"Hold on." He dug into his pocket and handed something to me. It was my phone. "Email your father and whoever else and tell them that you're working remotely for the time being."

"Okay but—" The look he gave could melt steel. As I pulled up my email, I said, "You need to explain what's going on. I'm tired of being left in the dark."

"Don't worry. I will once you send the email."

I did as he asked and then turned to him. "Did you find whoever tried to break in?"

"Yes."

I was shocked by his response. "Well? Did you turn them over to the police?"

"No, but they've been taken care of."

When he said that, I thought back to how bruised and bloody his fist had been and the smear of blood that had been on his face before we left the house.

He must have noticed that I put two and two together because he leaned over and said, "You don't have to worry about that guy anymore."

Unimaginable thoughts ran through my head and it was enough to get me to stop asking questions for the time being. Although it was warm in the car, a shiver crept through my body as realization hit me. Damien had no problem killing someone who crossed him. Would he have no issue doing the same to me? The thought caused a headache to form so I curled up as much as my seatbelt would allow and stared out the window. Some of the exhaustion, both mental and physical, had taken over my body and I fell into a restless sleep.

∼

"Where are we going?" I asked a while later. I was still groggy but feeling a bit more human as the SUV continued on its journey to who knew where.

"Upstate to a remote location that is more secure," Damien said. He had pulled out his laptop at some point and was now working on that as well. "Thought it would be nice to get out of the city for a bit and give my people enough time to clean up and add more security to my properties in the city."

I stopped my eyes from bulging out of my head. He had multiple properties in New York City? The townhouse we were staying in had to be worth about $13 million by itself. I glanced at my phone and saw that my father had replied. He wanted to talk to me, probably questioning my reason for working remotely.

"Will we be back by Christmas?" I tossed that question out there because Christmas was a week away and I wanted to be back with my family to celebrate it by then.

"Yes."

I sat back and got comfortable again and watched as we cruised down the highway to a place unknown by me. Thankfully, it wasn't long before we pulled up to a vast estate that seemed to go on for miles.

The enormous white home was something that dreams

were made of and the snow that lined the property made it look like something out of a movie. When Rob steered the car up the round driveway, I noticed a couple of black cars parked there too. *I was certain those were more security guards.*

"Do you own this house?" I asked Damien as the car came to a stop.

"No. My parents do."

"What? Why didn't you tell me we were going to your parents'?"

"Look, this is probably one of the most protected locations in the state outside of a government facility. This was the best option unless we flew out of the country. At least until we figure out who sent that asshole to the house."

"Did you tell your parents about all of this?"

Damien closed his laptop and placed it into his bag. "Yes, they know what happened and I told them about you. They split their time between the city and here, but they are here right now."

I played with my clothes. If he had mentioned it before, it would have given me an opportunity to at least look more presentable since I would be meeting his parents for the first time. Then again, why did this even matter? This wasn't real and would be over soon. He grabbed my hand, stopping my movements.

"Don't worry about what you're wearing. We are just going to go in there, we'll talk to my parents for a minute, and then we'll shower and change. Everyone understands what happened."

I quickly attempted to pull my hair into a ponytail, hoping that would make me look more put together. The doors on both sides of the car opened and I grabbed my purse and laptop bag. After I stepped out of the car, Damien followed suit and offered to hold my laptop bag as the two of us walked up the stairs to the home.

Someone had been expecting us because the door swung open and a man in a suit greeted us.

"Hello, sir."

Damien smiled back at him and this might have been the first time I had seen him smile. It was strange to see his lips turned up into a smile. He turned to me and said, "This is Bernard. Bernard, this is Anais."

"Nice to meet you." I held my hand out to shake his.

"It's nice to meet you too, Ms. Monroe." Before we could say anything further, a handsome couple entered the room. I could immediately tell that they were Damien's parents. It was easy to see that Damien got most of his looks and height from his father, and his eyes came from his mother.

"Oh, dear. You're okay, right?" The woman reached over and held Damien's face in her hands. "I swear I've been holding my breath until Rob pulled into the driveway."

"Everything is fine. We're safe and we're here now."

When she turned to me, she said, "You must be Anais. We've heard so much about you."

I gave a polite smile because that was news to me. I had barely heard anything about them and what I knew had come from Ellie's or my research. "Thanks for welcoming me into your home, Mrs. Cross."

"Of course! Any friend of Damien's is welcomed to our home, and please call me Selena. And this is my husband, Martin." She gave me a warm smile as Martin stuck his hand out to shake mine. "Do you need anything? I could have Maddie whip something up."

"Could she throw together something for breakfast? We haven't eaten."

"And when he hasn't eaten, he becomes harder to manage. Trust me I know this well." Selena smiled at me and faced her son.

"Sure, I can go do that and you'll show Anais to the Hampton guest room? That one should be ready. Damien, your room is still how you left it so that's where you'll be."

"Sounds great." He looked over at me before letting his eyes float back to his mother's and said, "I think Anais and I will probably change our clothes. We're wearing the clothes we've had on since last night."

"Right." Selena moved back and allowed us to move farther into the home. "I'll be in the kitchen or living room if you two need me."

"Damien, we should chat when you're done settling in," Martin said.

Although there was nothing that shouted out to me that something was up, I could tell that Martin's words had a different meaning to Damien than they did to me. The look he and his son shared told me that.

"Sounds good. I'll show Anais to her room."

Damien, Rob, and Bernard grabbed our things and we headed up the stairs and down a long hallway. It was lined with photos and paintings, most of which seemed to relate to the family in some sort of fashion, including photos and paintings of her children when they were small. When Damien stopped in front of one door, Rob and Bernard placed the bags they had been carrying down. Damien thanked them and the two went back the way we had come.

"So, you're right here," he said and opened the door he

was standing next to. The bedroom had all the standard amenities you'd expected in a guest room but was brighter and the complete opposite of the dark colors Damien seemed to stick to. The king-size bed had a beige comforter and a ton of pillows, and there was a dresser and windows that overlooked the huge backyard. The Crosses definitely took pride in having everything you could ever want. I was sure it would be a steep transition to go back to completely fending for myself.

"You have your own bathroom that is connected to your room."

"Wow. This home is beautiful. I can see why your parents wanted to live here."

"We have had some wonderful memories here." His tone was softer than his usual you-must-obey-my-orders tone. It made me want to dig deeper into his fond memories, but I knew he wouldn't respond.

"Well, I have to go get ready for a few conference calls, so I'll see you later."

I nodded as Damien turned away from me and I did the same. I walked farther into the guest bedroom after shutting the door behind me. Although I was tired of uprooting my life on a whim, I'd be staying here for a period of time and I needed to make the best of it.

I unpacked my things for what felt like the millionth time before walking into the bathroom and gasping. This bathroom belonged in a luxury suite of a hotel. The vast bathroom was big enough to fit my entire bedroom in it. Ridding my body of the clothes that had long since worn out their welcome, I turned the showerhead on to what I suspected was closer to hot than cold. I was right and when the water's temperature was where I wanted it, I stepped into the shower and almost swooned. Inside, the water beat down on my body and I felt as if I were under a warm, powerful waterfall. The force from the water felt so good, I could almost compare it to the massages that I had gotten when I stopped by Ellie's job for a session. I didn't know how long I had been in the shower when I swore that I saw something out of the corner of my eye and I was surprised to see Damien leaning on a door jamb. I cracked open the shower door and asked, "What are you doing here?"

"Just because we've switched locations doesn't mean the circumstances have changed. You belong to me and I get to do whatever I want."

"Even if that means interrupting a shower."

"Even that."

"Don't you have a conference call to get ready for? I wasn't expecting to see you for another few hours." I was looking forward to having some time alone, but I wasn't about to admit that out loud.

"When you're the boss, you can do whatever you want. Right now, my cock wants to get inside that smart mouth of yours and I'm happy to oblige."

21

DAMIEN

I closed the nightstand after stashing a box of condoms and walked to the bathroom. It would have taken no time for me to ditch my clothes at the door and enter the shower, but I didn't. I took my time removing them, letting the anticipation build because Anais didn't know what I was going to do. I kept my eyes on her naked form, thankful that Mom hadn't bothered to install frosted doors for this shower. Instead, the glass of the door was clear, allowing me to get as much of an eyeful as I wanted. Once I finished that task, I stepped into the shower.

"Get out of here. Can't even take a shower in peace." I didn't think she was trying that hard to fight me on this. It might have to do with her not being able to keep her eyes off my cock for longer than a second.

"I'll do you one better. You're going to suck my cock and you can sit on that marble bench right there and do it. No hurt knees, right?"

I could see an argument was at the tip of her tongue, but I preferred that something else was. She flipped her hair back and wiped the water from her eyes, and they landed on mine. I dipped my head, letting her know it was time. She drifted toward the bench before sitting on it and I could see her lick her lips as she came face-to-face with my dick. Her first move was to lick the head of my dick and I closed my eyes as I enjoyed the light sensation. Another lick almost made me buck my hips, hoping that she would take me deeper in her mouth.

As if she could read my mind, she took me in her mouth and gagged for a moment before she relaxed. She took me deeper than the previous time, realizing that she needed to relax her mouth in order to calm her gag reflex so that she could take more of me in. It worked. She took more of me and I could feel when my cock hit the back of her throat. I sucked in a deep breath and groaned in satisfaction.

She looked up at me as she was taking my cock and I nearly lost it. The feel of her mouth on me made my knees buckle slightly. Her tongue glided over the tip and alternated between that and taking my throbbing member into her mouth. Each time she started this cycle over again, she sucked my cock harder and I threw my head back with my eyes closed. She chuckled and that led to more vibrations heading straight to my dick. She moved her mouth back and sucked the head of my cock harder. I looked down at her again and the image was a lot for me to handle.

"I can't wait until you swallow every drop, Spitfire."

That and the fact that my hands had found their way into her hair seemed to give her a kick because she started enthusiastically alternating between sucking me deep, licking the head of my dick, and massaging my balls; all things that had me creeping closer and closer to the edge.

My hips moved involuntarily trying to get closer to her so she could take me even deeper than before. I groaned again before I took control over my body and plunged it in and out of her mouth. If I thought the image of her sucking me off was too much, seeing me pump my dick into her mouth was unbearable.

A roar preceded my orgasm and I watched as she made sure not to miss a drop. She looked up at me, a hint of a smile playing on her lips as she stood up and smirked.

"Now, I would appreciate it if you let me take a shower in peace." Her smirk betrayed the tone of her voice. I ignored her words and watched her for a moment before leaning down to pick up the shampoo and poured some of it into my hands. The light coconut fragrance hit my nostrils and I knew she must have smelt it too because she looked at me, water dripping down her face.

"Turn around."

She did as I asked without an argument and I placed my hands in her hair and began washing it, covering every inch. A low groan left Anais's lips as I massaged her scalp.

"Feels good?"

"You have no idea. Okay, I'm going to rinse this out and then you can do whatever you need to do under the showerhead."

"I'm getting out," I said, not offering an explanation. I knew it was time for a phone call that I needed to take, and this distraction took longer than I planned. I glanced at Anais and exited the shower. Her mouth was slightly open as she narrowed her gaze and turned away from me. I got a quick look at her ass, which was much appreciated, and grabbed a huge fluffy towel. I dried myself off and wrapped the towel around my waist before I grabbed my clothes and walked out of the bathroom.

It didn't take me long to get from Anais' room to my childhood room that had been revamped a couple of times since I had moved out. My parents kept the dark navy-blue color that I had liked as a teenager in the room but had changed some of the furniture out to flip it into a guest room if need be. Gone were the posters I'd hung on the wall, replaced by some of the paintings my mom had taken a liking to and wanted to be displayed in her home.

I tossed the clothes that I had been wearing previously into the hamper and checked the time on my phone. I had about twenty minutes until I had to be on a phone call that I didn't want to take. I threw on my trademark black suit and tie and styled my hair. I checked myself in the mirror and headed out the room and down to my father's office.

Of course, he was already there when I entered and briefly glanced at me before holding a finger up. He was on a call with a member of the board that I assumed would wrap up pretty soon.

"Thanks, Don. I'll talk to you later this week." Dad hung up the phone with a decisive click and stood up, grabbing his suit jacket, and putting it on.

"I thought we had a call with the twins and some potential organizations that wanted to expand their horizons in good old New York?"

Dad walked around his desk. "Change of plans. We're headed out and I'll explain it in the car."

22

ANAIS

After my shower, I looked for Damien, but didn't see him, so I went down to eat on my own. His mom joined me for only a moment then had a phone call she needed to take, and I didn't see her for the rest of the day. The evening was low-key, and I had to admit, I preferred it that way. I spent the evening alone, mostly resting and reading books on my phone. I thought Damien might come in and check on me, but he didn't. I was partially relieved and disappointed, but I didn't want to go seek him out. I went to bed early and felt rejuvenated the next morning. That was until I forced myself to text my father.

Me: *Hey Dad. I'm doing well. Just wanted to get away for a bit, but I should be back in time for Christmas.*

Dad: *Sounds good. Mom and I were worried about you.*

Me: *No need. Everything is fine and I'll see you soon.*

Dad: *Okay and don't forget to call your mother.*

I rolled my eyes but still sent a message back.

Me: *Will do.*

Once I rolled out of bed and was presentable, I headed

down to breakfast and found Selena in the dining room. It was bright with its white, beige, and gold décor and the similarly colored table sat fourteen. Selena matched the sophistication of the room with her black slacks, cream sweater, and her pinned-up hair. I wasn't shocked to see that Damien wasn't there. When we were back in his place in the city, he rarely was home for breakfast anyway. What was interesting was that Martin wasn't there either. I glanced at the chair next to me and sat down at the only other seat that had a placemat and utensils in front of it.

"Like father, like son. Am I right?" Selena smiled, which told me that she had read my mind and was used to the absences too. "I hope you don't mind that I had Maddie fix a few different dishes. I wasn't sure what you liked, and I forgot to ask you before we retired for the night."

"Oh, no, that's completely fine. I'm not a picky eater anyway, so I'm sure whatever you have will be fantastic."

She smiled at me again and made me wonder how Damien turned out to be the exact opposite of his mother in that regard. She was friendly whereas he was intimidating. Though, like his mother, Damien was caring. The way that he took care of me when someone broke into the townhouse, when he found me in the panic room, and how quickly he took charge to get us out of there. The way he made sure that I orgasmed during sex before him. These were just a few of the things that made me see him in a different light, and I wasn't sure how to feel about it.

"Did you sleep okay?"

"Ah, yes, I did. I slept like a baby." That was only partially true. I always had a hard time falling asleep when I was in an unfamiliar place and staying here was no different. When I did eventually get to sleep, it had been fine, but it was pointless to divulge all of that.

"That's good. I was hoping you would get some rest. I can only imagine how you must feel having had to deal with a break-in."

"Yeah, I wasn't expecting it and in addition to that, we aren't sure who did it." At least I wasn't sure. As soon as the words left my mouth, Maddie walked in with breakfast.

My stomach growled as I smelled the freshly cooked bacon that was sitting on the plate. Maddie also made Eggs Benedict and had cut up an assortment of fruit that she quickly retrieved from the kitchen once she left the hot foods for us to eat. She also brought out coffee. It seemed as if the coffee was an alarm because Martin and Damien walked into the room when she placed the hot pot in between Selena and me.

"Is there anything I can get you two?" Maddie asked, looking between Martin and Damien.

"We came in to get another cup of coffee and it seems like we were right on time," Martin said. That's when I realized that both of them had mugs in their hands.

"You could have rung me up and I would have brought it in there. That wouldn't have been a problem," Maddie replied.

"Coming in here wasn't a hardship. Trust me," Martin said as he strolled over to his wife and planted a kiss on her lips. Although he whispered his next words, I heard parts of it.

"How are you doing? I missed you this morning…" They continued to have a private conversation and to anyone looking on, you could see how much love and compassion was between them. Just watching as he gently massaged her shoulders as he spoke to her and the way her eyes lit up when she looked up at him. It almost made me wish that I could find the person to share that kind of connection with. I looked back down at my plate, feeling a little weird for having intruded on such a private moment between the two, before shoveling a forkful of eggs into my mouth.

"Ahem."

I almost forgot that Damien was there between watching the elder Crosses and deciding that food was the most important thing in this world right now.

"Yes?" I asked as I looked up at him.

"Did you have a good night's sleep?"

"I did. Thanks for asking."

"If you need anything, you know you can call—"

"Bernard," I said, finishing his sentence. "I know." Having a chef at Damien's house who came and cooked was weird. Getting used to having a butler that people repeatedly told me I could ask for help was weirder.

Damien gave me a peculiar look and walked around my chair and grabbed the hot pot of coffee. Martin leaned over and placed his mug near Damien's and Damien poured the coffee for both of them. They didn't linger around the dining room for much longer and once they both left I went back to eating the food.

"Mm-hmm," I said just as I grabbed my napkin from my lap and wiped my lips. "I need to go thank Maddie when we're done. This is so good."

"She always does such a good job. It's why I ask Martin to pay her whatever she wants because if she ever leaves, I don't know what we'll do. And he knows he didn't marry me for my cooking skills, and he could burn a pot just by boiling water. That literally happened when we were dating."

Thankfully, I hadn't eaten anything when she said that because the snort that I let out was so loud that it almost hurt. "That is hilarious."

She waited a moment before she asked, "What are you doing for the holidays?"

"I'll spend Christmas with my parents and then maybe go out with some friends for New Year's."

"That's what we usually do for Christmas too. Early in our marriage, I made Martin promise me that no matter what, he wouldn't work on Christmas. I wanted us to spend it together as a family and that was it. He's kept that promise every year. So that's what we do, and it has been ingrained into my boys' heads that unless something happens, everyone comes home for Christmas. I can't wait for them to bring their own families here too. We have so much room in this big house and I can't wait to fill it up with more of our extended family."

I said nothing about that as I took a sip of my coffee. I looked up from my plate and found Selena looking at me, before going back to eating her food. Was I reading too much into it or was she alluding to me? I had a feeling that me coming here might give Damien's parents the wrong idea, so it made me wonder why he had done so.

"You should make Damien bring you up here for our New Year's party. I know it's short notice, but I promise it will be a lot of fun. Plus, maybe it will make it more bearable for him. He, Broderick, and Gage have been trying to get out of the party for years because it's just a gathering of a bunch of stuffy suits, as Gage affectionately told me one year."

I chuckled. "Maybe I'll be able to make it." I couldn't

make Damien do a damn thing, but I'd let her live under the illusion that I could.

～

"I'M SO happy that you're spending some time with us."

"Thanks for having me," I said as I sat down in their great room, with the fireplace adding even more warmth to the room. Selena and I had been spending a great deal of time together over the last few days when I wasn't working because of Damien's and Martin's busy schedules. It included watching movies and television shows and doing a few workouts together in their home gym. We even got Maddie to teach us a few things in the kitchen, which both Selena and I appreciated. It was nice to socialize with someone in person. Just talking to Ellie and my parents on the phone or by text message and my coworkers by email had sucked.

Selena crossed her legs and said, "Sometimes it gets a little lonely because Martin works a lot. I have my projects that I do for charities here and there, but with it being winter and having poor weather more frequently, it makes it harder to get around. Sometimes some of our staff jokingly get offended when I try to help out. It's because I want to keep busy and I want that social interaction, you know?"

I couldn't believe that Selena was telling me this because we hadn't known each other for very long.

"I've also noticed some changes in Damien since you've been here, and it's been wonderful to see. There is a light back in his eyes that I haven't seen in a very long time."

I wondered where this conversation might head as I thought of what to say next. This might be the perfect opportunity to connect the pieces of the puzzle that had existed in my mind.

"What happened, if you don't mind me asking?"

"Hm?"

"What made him lose the light in his eyes?"

Selena stood up, adjusting the pretty pink cardigan she had worn today, and walked over to one of the many windows that lined the walls of the room. She looked outside for a moment before turning to look at me over her shoulder. "Some of us have heinous demons that continue to haunt us in everything we do. Some of us can move on and continue living life as we always have, but others have struggled to breathe because of the turmoil we have faced. I can't be the one to tell you what happened to Damien. It has to come from him."

I understood that. How could I have expected a mother to talk about her son behind his back?

"Tread lightly, my dear. I love my husband and sons very much, but I also know they've seen some things that no one should ever see. That has made them into the men they are today."

"Lunch is ready, Selena."

Selena looked toward the door and smiled.

"Thanks so much, Maddie." She looked back at me. "You don't want to know how many years it took her to drop 'Mrs. Cross.' That's my mother-in-law, rest her soul." Selena walked over to Maddie and turned to face me.

I got up and walked over to the other two women and together we went into the dining room to eat, but the questions in my mind remained.

23

DAMIEN

I let the water drip down my face, not caring if it painted an abstract pattern on my white T-shirt. I had just gotten back from the in-home gym my parents installed once they saw mine and was about to shower after a grueling workout. A text message notification on my phone from Kate, my publicist, was still running through my mind.

Kate: *The press is asking questions about Charlotte.*

As I turned the shower faucet on, my mind drifted to thoughts of what it was like growing up here. Being in this house brought back so many memories about my family, my childhood, and what used to be my life. The times that I would chase after Gage and Broderick after they entered my room when they weren't allowed when we were kids. Or the meals we would all share when Dad was home. Those times had been mostly great, but there were also the bad times that had colored in the lines of what made me into the man I am today.

The fire haunted my nightmares.

There was nothing I could do to stop the feeling that

came over me. I thought about the fact that I was the one who survived. She didn't. I was forced to leave Charlotte behind. Because who knew what kind of shit would have been written had my name been directly connected to the incident. At least that's what my father told me. When he practically threw me into the back seat of his car, and we sped down the empty road. I could remember hearing the sirens blaring in the background. But they weren't coming for us. They were coming to find Charlotte, the woman I had tried my damnedest to get out of the house, but it had been too late.

I remembered Dad pulling over on the side of a dark road miles and miles away from the fire. Tears welled in my eyes as my body hacked up the remnants of what was left in my stomach. He came over to me and gave me one pounding on the back.

Once I had stopped heaving, my father walked away and when I looked up, I saw him leaning on the hood of his car. I walked over and found him smoking one of his trademark cigars.

"Why didn't you let me go back and get Charlotte?" I had asked.

He tossed a glance my way before he shook his head. "Because then you both would have died. You're lucky that you happened to be downstairs and I could get you out in time."

"I don't feel lucky. I don't think I'll ever be able to get the fire—"

"I know, son. It will more than likely be etched in your mind forever."

I was upset. I wanted to mourn the life that had just been

lost, but nothing came out. No emotion. No tears. No wanting to break something. I felt almost...numb.

"Can I ask a question?"

"It's better if you don't."

I knew given some of the things I had overheard in the past that it was better to not ask questions, but this was something that was going to bother me for the rest of my life.

"I need to know the answer to this."

He took another puff of the cigar and said, "Go on."

"Did you have anything to do with that fire?"

I could see when Dad looked over at me and not even the darkness could hide the glare that was radiating from his eyes. I was fully expecting him to yell, which was rare, but he didn't.

"I had nothing to do with it. I was, however, tipped off that something was going to happen, and I clearly got there just in time." He put out his cigar and started walking toward the driver's-side door. "We need to get you home."

And that was the last time we ever spoke about what happened to Charlotte DePalma.

24

ANAIS

I adored the fact that the Cross estate also had a gym on its property. It gave me the opportunity to continue my workouts and not have to venture outside, which might cause a big distraction with security that needed to be involved. Plus, it was cold outside and if I could stay in the house that was what I was going to do.

About twenty minutes into my workout, I got a notification that Ellie had texted me. I waited until my workout was completed in ten minutes. During the last two minutes of my exercise routine, I had a flurry of text messages come through, making me wonder if something was wrong. During my five-minute cooldown, I picked up my phone and scanned the messages.

Ellie: *Hey?!*
Ellie: *Where are you?*
Ellie: *How are you?*
Ellie: *Is everything okay?*
Ellie: *Call me as soon as you can!*

Shit, I had forgotten to tell her that I was at Damien's

parents' house. I called her and the phone rang once before she picked up. She didn't say hello when she answered the phone.

"Is Damien there?"

Her question made me look around the room to verify what I already knew. No one was in the room with me. "No, he's not here. What's wrong?"

"Where are you?"

I noted that she still hadn't answered my question, further raising alarms in my mind. What was the meaning of all of this?

"At his parents' place, upstate."

"Why are you there?" The panic was clear in her voice, making me even more concerned.

I thought about telling Ellie what happened, but I was worried about dragging her into anything and causing her to worry. "A minor incident happened at Damien's place and he decided to spend a few days with his parents. Everything's fine." *Was it though? Was everything okay?*

The words that I said aloud made me remember just how much of this show Damien was running. I hadn't gotten a choice in whether or not we went to his parents'. I hadn't gotten the opportunity to talk about what had been going on, yet I was thrown into harm's way and had to hide in a panic room. Then while things were being investigated, I moved my life once again to be under lock and key in upstate New York. Hell, even the decision for me to enter this arrangement seemed predetermined because if I didn't, hundreds would have suffered. "What's going on?"

It felt as if I had asked that question for the billionth time, yet I was still no closer to finding out the answer. Almost everyone in my life seemed to operate several steps ahead of me while I was playing catch up. I was over it.

"There's more about Damien than you're aware of."

"Ellie, so help me if you don't start actually telling me what is going on, I'll—"

"I'm not sure how much there is to say because a lot of this is hearsay, but you need to find out who Charlotte DePalma is, what happened to her, and what Damien's involvement is in all of it."

"Who is Charlotte? What does she have to do with anything? Did something happen recently?"

"No, no, no. It was something that happened years ago, but I don't know exactly what. The press seems to be hinting around at it, but no one wants to be the first to say it. Probably fear of retribution."

"Okay, but what does this have to do with anything?"

Ellie waited a beat before she responded. "Stories have been circulating in the press that Damien is connected to Charlotte and that she died unexpectedly. I'm going to send you a few links to some stories. Is there any way we can find the rest of the money that is owed to Damien and give it to him? I don't know if he was involved or not, but I don't feel comfortable with you being up there with him and not closer to home."

Neither did I after all of this information was coming to light, and I couldn't stop myself from over-analyzing the situation as it all clicked into place almost simultaneously. Was Charlotte the actual reason he wanted to hide away at his parents' home for a few days? To give this time to blow over and to coordinate with his family on what the response would be? And why hadn't Damien told me anything about this? The startling realization that I was in way over my head shook me to my core. I did not know what I was facing and that terrified me.

∼

ANOTHER NIGHT, another fitful time of tossing and turning as I tried to get comfortable and fall asleep. But this time it was different. I was worried about whether I would survive to the end of this deal or not.

Now it was a fear. Fear of not knowing what Damien was capable of. Fear of losing what I had worked so hard for. Fear of not understanding Damien before I became addicted to him. I told myself I would not let myself become a victim of whatever game Damien was playing. The danger that seemed to grow as a result of me being connected to Damien was pretty damning as well. Although things felt somewhat more peaceful as time had gone on there was still the fact that I knew he was keeping things from me and it had nothing to do with being in a relationship. This was why I needed to turn any rational thoughts off and just get through the next few days because thirty days were almost done.

But there was more than that.

I knew that once day thirty came, I would never be the same. That was something that I would grapple with into the New Year.

A loud groan that turned into a scream made me sit up in bed and freeze. I looked at the door to the hallway. A thump followed and made me jump out of my skin and my first thought was that someone was trying to break into this house too. I got up and walked over to my door, knowing that that was the direction the noise had come from. I slowly opened the door and peeked into the hallway.

Nothing.

A few lamps provided some light in the dark abyss. I waited to see if I could hear anything else. It only took a few seconds, and I heard another groan that sounded like it came from Damien's room. I walked a few feet and then stood in front of the door before knocking softly. Although I didn't get an answer, I twisted the knob, and found the door unlocked. Telling myself that he needed help, I walked inside and found a dim room and a sight I never thought I would ever see.

Damien was sitting on the edge of his bed with his head in his hands, a single lamp illuminating both him and part of the room. I also saw what could have possibly made that loud thump—a huge book, just a few inches away from the end table that the lamp was on.

"Damien," I said, my voice just above a whisper. "Are you okay?"

"I thought I told you not to step foot in my bedroom at all? The rules from the city still apply here."

"But I thought you might—"

"Just leave."

Instead of doing as he asked, I walked farther into the room and stood in front of him, placing my hand on his shoulder. "Is there anything I can do to help?" I fully expected him to snap at me because I had once again disobeyed his orders, but what I saw was something more heartbreaking. He moved his hands from face. Although he wasn't crying, there was a lot of hurt in his eyes. Something felt special about this moment and I wondered if he shared this side of him with anyone else.

Something had replaced the hurt and anger that I felt toward him, something more intense that I couldn't quite place.

"Anais, go back to bed." His tone left no room for questioning, but it still sounded weaker than his normal terse commands.

"Okay, but feel free to come over if you need anything." I could tell that we were both shocked by the words that left my mouth because at the beginning of this arrangement, I wouldn't have said that. There was no way to take them back if I wanted to, and I didn't want to, which left me even more baffled.

I stumbled back to his door and closed it behind me and walked back across the hall to my bedroom. I knew the chances of me getting back to sleep were slim, but one of the burning questions that had been on my mind had been answered. If he was having trouble sleeping, it made sense why he didn't want to sleep in the same room as me. I wondered if the secrets to the demons he fought at night lay in the room where he went to sleep.

I drifted in and out of sleep when I heard a creaky sound from across the room. "Who's there?"

"It's me." My body recognized his voice immediately. I listened carefully as his feet shuffled along the floor as he made his way to my bed.

"What are you doing here?" I whispered once he was standing over me.

"Getting into bed."

I was thankful for the darkness that surrounded us

because he would have seen my jaw hit the floor. He climbed into the bed and did as he usually did when he was in a space: took over. But I had no problem with it because he wrapped me up in his embrace. Together we fell asleep, and I hoped that whatever had woken him up would remain in the depths of the shadows so that he could get some rest.

25

DAMIEN

The next morning, I awoke and was taken aback when I didn't find myself in my childhood bedroom. It took my eyes a moment to adjust and the first thing that hit my nostrils was a subtle smell of coconut.

Anais.

Her hair smelled like the shampoo that she used while staying here. Visions of what had occurred last night and her finding me in a vulnerable state didn't sit well with me. She caught the end of what sometimes happens when Charlotte's memory haunted me in my sleep. This was never supposed to happen, and I had always been careful not to let anyone know what transpired when I closed my eyes to sleep.

After she checked on me, I'd felt compelled to go to her. Once I stepped into her room, I couldn't stop myself from crawling into her bed. When I was next to her, it didn't take long for me to pass out between the soft cream sheets. Although I had been woken up in the middle of the night, it was the most rested I had felt in a long time. Rejuvenated in a way that I hadn't expected.

Anais was lying on her side with her back toward me. I shifted my arm that was around her waist and dragged my finger along the smooth skin that had become exposed during the night. She stirred, and I didn't feel an ounce of guilt about it.

In the early morning light, I watched as she turned to face me, a smile playing on her lips that made me stop and stare. She mumbled something that I didn't catch, stirring as she fought between being awake and staying asleep. My cock hardened against the pajamas pants I was wearing.

"I want you. Right now." My voice came out more gruff than normal, something I barely recognized.

"I'm not saying no."

"But are you saying yes?"

"Yes."

That one word set all things in motion. I turned her head toward me and claimed her lips. She turned her body so that she was now lying on her back, making it easier for me to deepen the kiss. My hands slid down her sides to the waistband of the short shorts she had worn to bed. She held her breath as my hand made its way to her mound. I smirked at what I found.

"Either you were having a pleasurable dream or that kiss was as hot for you as it was for me."

"I plead the fifth."

I swallowed a retort when I felt how wet she was. She helped me remove her pajama shorts and underwear and I started playing with her nub before I pushed a finger into her cunt.

"You know what I can't wait for? To take this ass."

I said it to get a reaction out of her and I got one. She threw her head back and moaned and my cock was rock hard against her hip. I didn't know if that was because of the sex-induced haze she was currently in, but we could address that later.

"Flip back onto your side with your back to me again."

While she got back into position, I stood up and took the condom out of the nightstand, thanking myself for having the foresight to think of it. It took no time for me to rid myself of my pants and placed the condom on my erection prior to running my cock up and down her slit.

"I like when you do that."

"I know," I responded as I entered her. I closed my eyes briefly, enjoying the feeling of her tight walls around my cock. One day I wanted to know what it felt like to have no barriers between us.

Entering her from this angle was a fresh experience for the both of us together as my hands alternated between fondling her breasts and her clit.

"Yes," she hissed out, voicing the same sensations that were going through my body. Every time my cock drove into her, I wondered when this would be it. When this would get old. When I would want to cut this off. Those thoughts vanished the closer we got to our peaks. It didn't take long for both of us to reach our climaxes, her going before me. We took a moment to catch our breath and then I pulled out of her, almost immediately regretting the motion.

"That was a way to wake up," Anais said as I felt her turn to face me.

My eyes were closed as I stopped to enjoy the euphoria I

felt after the high came down. "That it was," I said, but she didn't respond. Instead, I felt her snuggle deeper into my chest and play with some of the hair on my happy trail. Something had been swirling in my head, just before I woke her up by pleasuring her. I debated whether or not I wanted to say anything. The silence around us was so peaceful. I didn't want to do anything to jeopardize it.

"Damien?" she asked.

I opened my eyes and looked down at her. "Yes?"

She looked stunning in the pale light that the sun was casting on the room, with her hair sprayed out across the pillow behind my arm. This was a sight I could get used to seeing on a regular basis. I expected myself to flinch at the thought because of the events that transpired with Charlotte. I thrived on remaining single and dating when I wanted, but this felt different. And I didn't know if thirty days were going to be enough. She was going to be mine, period.

"Do you want to talk about what happened last night?"

And just like that, ice-cold water surged through my veins as I shifted my body to get from underneath her. "No. I don't want to discuss it."

"But I thought—"

"You thought wrong," I said as I got up and out of bed. I put on the pajama pants that I had worn when I entered and walked toward the door. No one needed to know the pain that that night had caused, and I wasn't ready to talk about.

I didn't look back even when I heard her sniffle and the barrier between us closed with a soft click.

26

ANAIS

"I'm an idiot," I mumbled to myself as I paced my bedroom. After Damien stormed out of my room, we had done our best to avoid one another over the last couple of days, which hadn't been hard due to us both claiming the work we needed to do for our jobs was more of a priority than anything else.

It was two days before Christmas. I felt like a mouse in a glass prison that needed to get the hell out. I knew going into this there was a chance that I might become addicted to him. His touch. The way he made me feel. Him allowing me into parts of his world. I thought I'd done my best to prevent it. When Damien didn't want me, I avoided being near him, but even that hadn't protected me and my thoughts from migrating to him.

I had done what I said I wasn't going to do. I was addicted to Damien Cross and it was only a matter of time before he realized it and kicked me to the curb. The thought of him doing that made my stomach turn. I knew who he was before I became addicted and yet I still fell. No, I needed to get out of whatever this was first. He didn't even trust me enough to tell me what caused him to scream out at night. I could try to make it through the last week, but I knew I would be lying to myself and driving myself to the point of hysteria if I stayed. I also wasn't any closer to finding out who Charlotte DePalma was or her connection to Damien. This all troubled me and was why I needed to leave now.

There was another way that I could find out more information about Charlotte. I stared at my computer, lying on the made-up bed in this room. Ellie had done some research when she alerted me but hadn't found much at the time. Over the last couple of days, I hadn't been able to find anything and it didn't hurt to look things up one more time, did it?

I opened my laptop, typed in my password, and waited for my browser to load. Once it had, I typed in Charlotte's name and New York City to see if anything popped up. I got lucky because an article that was published four hours ago came up. My hand shook as my cursor hovered over the link. I took a deep breath and clicked. My eyes scoured the article, taking in every word about an event that took place years ago. An arsonist burned down a cabin, killing one person: Charlotte DePalma. The murder was tragic, but one of the pictures that was included with the article was an image of a younger Damien. It had been easy to spot, outside of him looking much like the man he was today, because of the pictures Selena had hanging around her home. He was listed as Charlotte's boyfriend and the last person she was seen with although he was never charged with a crime. My emotions jumped from sadness, to fear, to anger more rapidly than I could deal with. This needed to end.

I figured Damien was either in his childhood bedroom or in his father's office, and since I hoped to catch him alone, I walked across the hall to his bedroom first.

A quick knock on the door confirmed that he wasn't in there, so I went downstairs to the office, hoping that both Damien and his father weren't in there. I knocked on the study door.

"Come in." It was Damien's voice.

I took a deep breath to steel myself because I hadn't been expecting him to be there, and I was about to face the devil himself.

I opened the door and he looked over at me from his place at one of the windows behind the huge wooden desk. He was alone. "Is this urgent? I have a phone call in five minutes with some important investors who are overseas."

"Who is Charlotte DePalma?" I wanted to give him an opportunity to explain himself, although I knew way more than he thought I did. I walked further into the room and stood several steps in front of him.

"Why do you care?"

"What happened to her?" I believed this was the first time since Damien and I had met that I had shocked him. His eyes widened briefly yet an indifferent expression moved into place.

"You need to mind your business," Damien said, still as calm as ever. That only further enraged me.

"I'll tell you who Charlotte DePalma is. Charlotte DePalma is your ex-girlfriend who died in a horrible house fire when you were eighteen."

His silence was palpable.

"Wow." Damien's silence spoke volumes. When he still

hadn't said anything, I continued, "Why didn't you tell me about any of this?"

"It wasn't your concern nor your business."

Tears welled up in my eyes and it finally became clear to me where I stood in all of this and how much I had truly fallen.

"This whole time you were hiding this from me."

"Anais, this wasn't any—"

"Stop with the bullshit!"

His blue eyes darkened, and I could feel their stare trying to freeze me into place. "Watch your words. Unless you want me to punish you by—"

"You can go fuck yourself." Any threat that he had behind his words didn't mean a thing to me at this point as I unleashed the pent-up anger and frustration that had been inside of me for far too long. "Did you have her killed?"

Damien's demeanor turned hard. "I don't have to explain myself to you."

"What? She didn't want to play any of your little games, was that it? Is that why you did it?"

"You have no idea what you're talking about."

"I know I wasn't there fifteen years ago, but what I do know is that you still won't tell me the truth and you locked me in a deal that I had no choice to be in."

"Bullshit, Anais. You always had a choice. You could have walked away at any point, and I would have let you go." Damien took two steps toward me.

I scoffed. "No, the whole point was to use me until you got tired of me. If I left, my family's company would have gone to shit, and you wouldn't have given a damn about it. That's because you care about no one but Damien Cross."

My words had their intended effect on Damien because he stopped walking toward me. "Well, the opportunity to leave is still open."

"Does that mean you'll still wipe my father's debt? That's the only reason I'm here." The taste of freedom was almost too much to bear.

"Given the number of days that you've been here and seeing that there is only a week left, if your father pays the rest of the money that your services didn't provide, the debt will be wiped."

I knew he used that phrasing to get under my skin. It did sting, but I didn't care. I prayed my father had that money and it wasn't my problem anymore.

"This whole arrangement is over, and I don't care if the thirty days aren't up. As someone who said that they would always keep their word, I trust that you will wipe my father's debt clean once he pays off the rest of what I couldn't as it states in the contract."

Damien took a step back and looked out the window in his chair. "Pack your things and I'll make sure that Rob drops you back off at your apartment."

"Thank you," I said, and turned and walked away. I could feel his eyes burning a hole through my body. And it wasn't until I closed his office door behind me that I wiped the tears that were flying down my face.

I bolted up the stairs and reached the room that had become my second home. It didn't take long for me to pack the items that I'd brought with me and once I was ready, I carried my bags down the stairs. I felt bad for leaving under such short notice and after Selena and I had gotten friendly with one another, but I didn't think I could face her at the moment. Bernard greeted me at the door and wished me well on my trip back to the city.

I thanked him and he opened the door just as Rob was exiting the car. The two men helped load the few bags I had, and I gave a sad smile to Bernard. I stepped across the threshold to enter the waiting car that would soon take me back to the life I once knew.

∼

ALTHOUGH ALIVE AND BUSTLING, New York City's streets seemed lonely even as we passed hundreds of people. It wasn't long before Rob dropped my bags off at the door of my apartment and gave me a small wave. He walked back down the stairs and into his car. It took me a minute to find my keys, since I hadn't used them in about a month.

Once I walked inside, I felt that loneliness creep up again. Ellie was at work so there was no one to greet me at the door like there had been at the Cross residence. Although I had been renting this apartment for three years, it was like entering a new home for the first time. This didn't feel like me anymore. It wasn't the place I used to know, although everything looked the same. It wasn't the apartment that had changed. It was me.

27

ANAIS

"Thanks for coming over for dinner."

I smiled at my mom as she grabbed my hand and squeezed. There was a lighter expression on her face, one that I hadn't seen in quite some time.

"Of course, it's Christmas. Where else would I be?" We both chuckled as Dad joined us at the dining room table.

My father cleared his throat. "There's something I wanted to tell both of you."

My hand immediately went to grab my wine glass, bracing for the worst.

"The debt is fully paid."

I was glad that I hadn't taken the opportunity to take a sip because I knew it would have ended up everywhere.

"What?" My mother was the first to speak.

My father nodded. "Looks like there was a Christmas miracle. I wasn't expecting the call at all since I still had a couple of weeks to pay it, but the entire thing has been wiped clean. I didn't have to pay a cent."

Wow, Damien hadn't even charged my father what he and I had agreed would be paid before I stormed out of his parents' home. I was stunned, yet ecstatic about the news, but I wondered what the catch was because it seemed as if Damien never gave up on anything without a fight.

"To make matters better, this officially puts Monroe Media Agency back in the black and clients are coming back in droves. I think—no, I know—things are going to be much better." He hugged my mom first and then reached over to hug me.

"That's wonderful news, Dad. I'm so happy. Sounds like drinks are on you tonight."

My parents chuckled and we enjoyed the rest of our Christmas evening.

∼

THE CHRISTMAS HOLIDAY came and went, and the next few days flew by in a blur. It didn't take long for me to get back into a similar routine that I had before Damien came into my life. I went to work, and I came home, and the same thing happened the next day. Ellie and I hung out a few times, but life got in the way once more and it wasn't as frequent as both of us wanted it to be. Damien hadn't said a word to me since I left, and word never got out about our arrangement or fake relationship rumors. The talk about Charlotte also died down around the same time and I wondered if he had something to do with that. To top it all off, I had found nothing else about the man who was watching me, nor the break-in at the townhouse. At the very least, he seemed as if he wasn't watching me anymore and for that I was grateful.

New Year's Eve and Day came and went, and I thought about the Cross family more often than I wanted to admit. Although it wasn't my style, I would have liked to have been there to support Selena, especially given how nice she had been to allow me to stay in her home.

On the job front, work was going well. Monroe Media Agency was still gaining new clients and I could see the stress leaving my father's face as the days went on. I couldn't be more thrilled. I was busy with the new clients too.

A couple of days after New Year's, I was reading an email from a coworker when my father stepped into the office after knocking on the door.

"Hey, what's up?"

"Your mother can't make it to a meet-and-greet event tonight. Could you join me?"

I looked down at the several-years-old-but-still-in-good-shape black A-line dress I was wearing and looked back at my father.

"What you're wearing is fine because it's not a huge formal affair. Plus, it's been a while since you and I have had some father-daughter time anyway."

I put my head on my fist as I leaned on my desk. "Dad, if you wanted to hang out, we could hang out."

"I know and I think we should do more of that. Things are looking up and we're both going to have more free time to do more with one another, your mother included. She and I have a date set for Friday night."

I smiled. I was glad they were still going out and keeping the romance alive. "And did she give you that fancy Rolex that you have on your arm?"

Dad actually blushed and nodded but didn't offer an explanation.

"Yeah, I'm not doing anything tonight so I can go with you."

"Perfect. I'll see you at five and we can walk over together."

"Sounds good. See you then." We shared a small smile, and he left my office, closing the door behind him.

⁓

"That wasn't so bad, was it?"

He was right. The event had been fine, and we spent most of the time talking up Monroe Media Agency to some of his friends and potential clients. Plus, I got to spend time with my father and have a glass of wine. What more could I ask for?

I glanced at my father and said, "No, it was fine. You know I'm not a huge fan of schmoozing."

"But you're wonderful at it. And you've definitely gotten better with it over the last couple of months."

"Thanks, Dad."

We walked over to get our coats that had been checked and I smiled when Dad helped me put mine on. We walked over to the exit of the building where the fundraiser was being held and looked around. "Do you want to go home with me so you can see your mother? Then I can drop you off at your place or you can stay in your old room."

"Sure. We can split a cab."

"Okay, I'll see if there's one nearby. You stay near the

building and keep warm." His suggestion made sense. It was still cold in the city and standing near the building would probably be warmer. Plus, this street wasn't well lit, and I appreciated being closer to a source of light, versus trying to find a cab in the dark.

Only seconds later shots rang out and I dropped to the ground so fast I lost every ounce of breath that had been in my lungs. Chaos surrounded me as people ran in different directions, trying to outrun whoever was firing the gun.

Although my ears were still ringing, my first thought was finding out where Dad was. "Dad?"

I didn't get a response.

"Dad!" My scream was more of a shriek as I panicked and tried to pick myself off of the ground.

It took me a moment, but I saw a motionless body lying a small distance away and I took a few steps toward the body, shoving people who were running toward me out of the way. It was then that my eyes landed on the watch, the one I had complimented my father on just hours before.

"No, Dad!" I screamed as I tried to run toward him. I could see something dark seeping out from underneath him and the urge to get to him increased tenfold. My forward mobility stopped when someone grabbed me from behind and covered my mouth. My muffled screams did not attract any attention as people ducked for cover.

"Get off of me! Let me go!" came out as a mumbled mess, and the person continued to pull me in the opposite direction of where I wanted to go. It was then that I was thrown into the back of an SUV that then sped off. When I tried to sit up and open the door, the childproof locks were engaged in one swift motion and the next thing I knew, something was thrown over my head and my hands were tied behind my back. My screams did nothing to deter my kidnappers and the SUV sped off to its destination unbeknownst to me.

∽

THANK YOU FOR READING! The next book in the series, Scarred Empire, will be released soon.

ABOUT THE AUTHOR

Bri loves a good romance, especially ones that involve a hot anti-hero. That is why she likes to turn the dial up a notch with her own writing. Her Broken Cross series is her debut dark romance series.

She spends most of her time hanging out with her family, plotting her next novel, or reading books by other romance authors.

https://www.facebook.com/briblackwoodwrites

ALSO BY BRI BLACKWOOD

Broken Cross Series

Sinners Empire (Prequel)

Savage Empire

Scarred Empire

Steel Empire

Made in United States
Cleveland, OH
30 December 2024

Made in United States
Cleveland, OH
30 December 2024